TOEIC

練習測驗（9）

聽力錄音QR碼（1~100題）

LISTENING TEST

In the Listening test, you will be asked to demonstrate how well you understand spoken English. The entire Listening test will last approximately 45 minutes. There are four parts, and directions are given for each part. You must mark your answers on the separate answer sheet. Do not write your answers in your test book.

PART 1

Directions: For each question in this part, you will hear four statements about a picture in your test book. When you hear the statements, you must select the one statement that best describes what you see in the picture. Then find the number of the question on your answer sheet and mark your answer. The statements will not be printed in your test book and will be spoken only one time.

Statement (C), "They're sitting at a table," is the best description of the picture, so you should select answer (C) and mark it on your answer sheet.

1.

2.

GO ON TO THE NEXT PAGE

3.

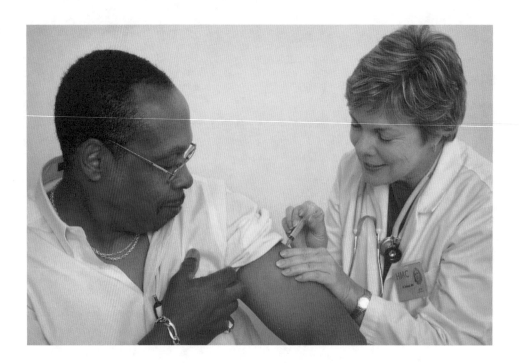

4.

5.

6.

GO ON TO THE NEXT PAGE

Directions: You will hear a question or statement and three responses spoken in English. They will not be printed in your test book and will be spoken only one time. Select the best response to the question or statement and mark the letter (A), (B), or (C) on your answer sheet.

7. Mark your answer on your answer sheet.

8. Mark your answer on your answer sheet.

9. Mark your answer on your answer sheet.

10. Mark your answer on your answer sheet.

11. Mark your answer on your answer sheet.

12. Mark your answer on your answer sheet.

13. Mark your answer on your answer sheet.

14. Mark your answer on your answer sheet.

15. Mark your answer on your answer sheet.

16. Mark your answer on your answer sheet.

17. Mark your answer on your answer sheet.

18. Mark your answer on your answer sheet.

19. Mark your answer on your answer sheet.

20. Mark your answer on your answer sheet.

21. Mark your answer on your answer sheet.

22. Mark your answer on your answer sheet.

23. Mark your answer on your answer sheet.

24. Mark your answer on your answer sheet.

25. Mark your answer on your answer sheet.

26. Mark your answer on your answer sheet.

27. Mark your answer on your answer sheet.

28. Mark your answer on your answer sheet.

29. Mark your answer on your answer sheet.

30. Mark your answer on your answer sheet.

31. Mark your answer on your answer sheet.

Directions: You will hear some conversations between two people. You will be asked to answer three questions about what the speakers say in each conversation. Select the best response to each question and mark the letter (A), (B), (C), or (D) on your answer sheet. The conversation will not be printed in your test book and will be spoken only one time.

32. Where do the speakers most likely work?
(A) At a custom print shop.
(B) At a construction site.
(C) In a bakery.
(D) In an appliance store.

33. What problem does the man mention?
(A) A shipment was delayed.
(B) An order was cancelled.
(C) An employee was late to work.
(D) A machine was not cleaned properly.

34. What will happen this afternoon?
(A) A business will close.
(B) An order will be completed.
(C) A repair person will arrive.
(D) An event will be set up.

35. Where are the speakers?
(A) In a parking garage.
(B) In a restaurant.
(C) In a movie theater.
(D) In a bank.

36. What does the man decide to do?
(A) Withdraw money from a cash machine.
(B) Call a customer service number.
(C) Make a payment online.
(D) Return at a later time.

37. What will be sent to the man?
(A) A confirmation number.
(B) A warranty offer.
(C) An account statement.
(D) A VIP membership card.

38. What is the woman coordinating?
(A) A company outing.
(B) A grand opening.
(C) A new employee orientation.
(D) An annual performance review.

39. Where do the speakers most likely work?
(A) At a travel agency.
(B) At a department store.
(C) At business school.
(D) At a bank.

40. What does the woman say she will do?
(A) Book a venue.
(B) Prepare a contract.
(C) Find a substitute.
(D) Cancel an order.

41. Where is the conversation taking place?
(A) At a library.
(B) At a museum.
(C) At a theater.
(D) At a supermarket.

42. Why does the woman apologize?
(A) A website is not accessible.
(B) An event has been canceled.
(C) Some tickets are unavailable.
(D) Some prices have increased.

43. What does the man say he will do next?
(A) Call a manager.
(B) Register a complaint.
(C) Go to a different location.
(D) Visit a website.

GO ON TO THE NEXT PAGE

44. Where is the conversation taking place?
- (A) At a travel agency.
- (B) In a hotel.
- (C) In an airport.
- (D) At a restaurant.

45. According to the woman, what will the men receive?
- (A) A seating upgrade.
- (B) A discount voucher.
- (C) A parking permit.
- (D) A travel guidebook.

46. What will the men most likely do next?
- (A) Give a presentation.
- (B) Eat at a restaurant.
- (C) Return to their workplace.
- (D) Change the hotel reservation.

---

47. What does the man mean by, "So…the accounting expense proposal"?
- (A) He wants to know if a document is ready.
- (B) He wants to extend a deadline.
- (C) He wants to know if schedule has been changed.
- (D) He wants an explanation for a policy decision.

48. What does the woman say about an expense estimate?
- (A) It has been misplaced.
- (B) It will be higher than expected.
- (C) It was already approved.
- (D) It contained some mistakes.

49. What will the man discuss at a meeting?
- (A) Contracts with vendors.
- (B) Design modifications.
- (C) Accounting practices.
- (D) Candidates for a career promotion.

---

50. What problem does the woman mention?
- (A) Parking in the area is limited.
- (B) The sales forecast is negative.
- (C) Customer complaints have increased.
- (D) Bad weather has been predicted.

51. What does the man say he will decide this evening?
- (A) When to launch a new sales promotion.
- (B) When to meet with investors.
- (C) Whether the store will be closed.
- (D) Whether additional employees should be hired.

52. What does the woman offer to help the man with?
- (A) Organizing a carpool.
- (B) Revising a work schedule.
- (C) Contacting employees.
- (D) Opening the store.

---

53. What does the woman ask the man about?
- (A) The price of an item.
- (B) The location of a store.
- (C) The maker of a product.
- (D) The availability of colors.

54. Why does the man say, "Those are nice"?
- (A) To convince a friend to buy headphones.
- (B) To suggest an alternative product.
- (C) To compliment a co-worker.
- (D) To express agreement.

55. What does the man say he will do?
- (A) Find a comparable item.
- (B) Check a price list.
- (C) Print a receipt.
- (D) Provide a coupon code.

---

56. Why is the man calling?
  (A) To schedule a repair.
  (B) To inquire about a bill.
  (C) To check the status of an order.
  (D) To provide an updated credit card number.

57. What problem does the woman mention?
  (A) A product was sent to the wrong address.
  (B) A product is no longer available.
  (C) A deadline was missed.
  (D) A credit card payment was not received.

58. What does the woman offer to do?
  (A) Speak with a supervisor.
  (B) Issue a refund.
  (C) Change a password.
  (D) Add a warranty.

---

59. What is the conversation mainly about?
  (A) Finding a guest speaker for a convention.
  (B) Creating an employee handbook.
  (C) Organizing a training session.
  (D) Preparing for a business exposition.

60. What does the man suggest doing?
  (A) Reserving more time.
  (B) Revising a timetable.
  (C) Sending out invitations.
  (D) Making a brochure.

61. What does Sophia say she is concerned about?
  (A) A canceled reservation.
  (B) An unconfirmed meeting.
  (C) An approaching deadline.
  (D) An incorrect report.

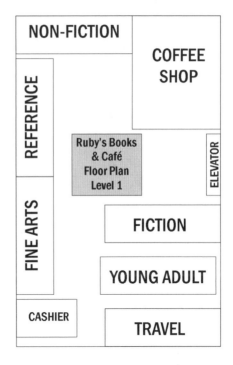

62. Who most likely is the man?
  (A) A sales clerk.
  (B) A baker.
  (C) An author.
  (D) A teacher.

63. What does the woman say she heard about the book?
  (A) It will provide opportunities for discussion.
  (B) It is the first book in a series.
  (C) It has been a best-seller for many months.
  (D) It was written by an associate.

64. Look at the graphic. In which section is the book that the woman is looking for?
  (A) Travel.
  (B) Reference.
  (C) Non-fiction.
  (D) Young Adult.

GO ON TO THE NEXT PAGE.

Silk Road Restaurant Rating

Atmosphere
✪ ✪ ✪ ✪
Prices and value
✪ ✪
Customer service
✪ ✪ ✪ ✪ ✪
Menu options
✪ ✪ ✪

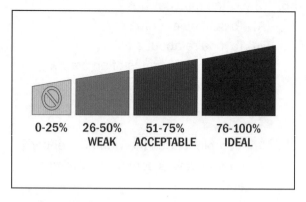

0-25% 26-50% 51-75% 76-100%
          WEAK   ACCEPTABLE   IDEAL

65. Who is the man?
(A) An editor.
(B) A manager.
(C) A financial consultant.
(D) A food critic.

66. Look at the graphic. What area does the woman want the restaurant to improve in?
(A) Customer service.
(B) Menu options.
(C) Atmosphere.
(D) Prices and value.

67. What does the man mean when he says, "They may be willing to make a few compromises"?
(A) The owners may agree to lower prices.
(B) The owners may wish to expand the business.
(C) The critics may welcome another visit.
(D) The staff may appreciate the time off.

68. What event is taking place?
(A) A sales meeting.
(B) An award ceremony.
(C) A training session.
(D) A weather forecast.

69. What does the man ask about?
(A) Additional safety procedures.
(B) Different lab facilities.
(C) Experiment results.
(D) Alternative power sources.

70. Look at the graphic. According to the woman, how many bars will be displayed when the battery should be replaced?
(A) Three bars.
(B) Two bars.
(C) One bar.
(D) Zero bars.

Directions: You will hear some talks given by a single speaker. You will be asked to answer three questions about what the speaker says in each talk. Select the best response to each question and mark the letter (A), (B), (C), or (D) on your answer sheet. The talks will not be printed in your test book and will be spoken only one time.

71. According to the speaker, what will be changing at the company?
 (A) How drivers' hours are scheduled.
 (B) How drivers are tracked.
 (C) How customer complaints are handled.
 (D) How reservations are submitted.

72. What will the company be able to do for customers?
 (A) Reduce wait times.
 (B) Extend service routes.
 (C) Lower prices.
 (D) Offer more products.

73. What will Ms. Eastman be doing?
 (A) Conducting a survey.
 (B) Inspecting vehicles.
 (C) Testing equipment.
 (D) Training employees.

74. What business is the speaker calling?
 (A) A dentist's office.
 (B) A shoe repair shop.
 (C) A transportation service.
 (D) A travel agency.

75. Why did the speaker take a taxi?
 (A) He was concerned about parking.
 (B) He was late for a dinner date.
 (C) His car broke down.
 (D) His train never arrived.

76. What would the speaker like to know?
 (A) How to get to an event.
 (B) Whether a schedule has changed.
 (C) When a new service will begin.
 (D) How much a membership will cost.

77. Who most likely is the speaker?
 (A) A real estate agent.
 (B) A legal advisor.
 (C) An architect.
 (D) A banker.

78. What does the speaker say is a problem?
 (A) Some construction has not been completed.
 (B) A warehouse is difficult to find.
 (C) An inspection will be postponed.
 (D) A price is higher than desired.

79. What does the speaker ask the listener to do?
 (A) Submit a deposit.
 (B) Sign a waiver.
 (C) Return the call promptly.
 (D) Review a document carefully.

80. What is the main topic of the broadcast?
 (A) A celebrity interview.
 (B) A weather report.
 (C) A traffic update.
 (D) An international news story.

81. According to the speaker, what will begin today?
 (A) A sports tournament.
 (B) A music festival.
 (C) A conference.
 (D) A seasonal market.

82. What does the speaker suggest that listeners do?
 (A) Arrive early.
 (B) Bring warm clothes.
 (C) Purchase tickets online.
 (D) Take public transportation.

GO ON TO THE NEXT PAGE

83. Who most likely is the speaker?
(A) A computer programmer.
(B) A personnel manager.
(C) An accountant.
(D) A real estate agent.

84. What does the speaker mean when she says, "The deadline to submit was May 15"?
(A) They missed a good hiring opportunity.
(B) They need to verify some details.
(C) They must move forward with a task.
(D) They forgot to notify a colleague.

85. According to the speaker, what will happen next week?
(A) A policy will be implemented.
(B) Interviews will begin.
(C) Bonuses will increase.
(D) A system upgrade will be completed.

86. What is Corona Flash?
(A) A store security system.
(B) An Internet service provider.
(C) A teleconferencing application.
(D) A new brand of smartphone.

87. What does the speaker mean when he says, "Teleconferencing should be easy and a conferencing company should be honest"?
(A) Employees need more training.
(B) Networks should be faster.
(C) An invoice should be reviewed.
(D) Other systems are not as efficient.

88. What does the speaker say listeners can do on a website?
(A) Register a product.
(B) Make a purchase.
(C) View a demonstration.
(D) Sign up for updates.

89. What did the *Cleveland Daily News* recently do?
(A) It announced award winners.
(B) It merged with another newspaper.
(C) It reviewed a group of restaurants.
(D) It reduced its subscription fee.

90. What has the business done recently?
(A) Bought a new property.
(B) Leased a larger facility.
(C) Hired more staff.
(D) Upgraded some computers.

91. What does the speaker imply when he says, "There are new firms opening every day"?
(A) A branch location will be built.
(B) Competition for customers will increase.
(C) More people will move to the area.
(D) Road conditions will worsen.

92. Where is the announcement taking place?
(A) At a catering company headquarters.
(B) At a sports stadium.
(C) At a shopping mall.
(D) At a restaurant.

93. What does the speaker say will happen immediately after today's event?
(A) Experts will provide consultations.
(B) Attendees will fill out a survey.
(C) A famous chef will speak.
(D) A meal will be served.

94. What does the speaker say about Uptown Pantry?
(A) It has won an award.
(B) It has undergone a renovation.
(C) It is now officially open.
(D) It is giving away free tickets.

BAKERY ITEM	# of votes
Muffin	503
Éclair	411
Scone	392
Doughnut	225
Cupcake	144

Late Payment Policy	
Days Overdue	Fee
5	$5.99
10	$12.98
15	$21.97
20	$30.96

95. Look at the graphic. Which item will be discounted this week?
(A) Cupcake.
(B) Doughnut.
(C) Scone.
(D) Muffin.

96. Why does the speaker thank Daniel?
(A) He proposed a sales promotion.
(B) He developed new bakery items.
(C) He worked extra hours.
(D) He submitted an order.

97. What does the speaker remind the listeners to do?
(A) Make some suggestions.
(B) Sign up for a task.
(C) Clean some equipment.
(D) Count customer votes.

98. Where does the speaker most likely work?
(A) At a financial institution.
(B) At a water park.
(C) At a utility company.
(D) At a bank.

99. Look at the graphic. How much is the Listener's late fee?
(A) $5.99.
(B) $12.98.
(C) $21.97.
(D) $30.96.

100. What must the listener provide to sign up for a service?
(A) A medical certificate.
(B) An identification card.
(C) Some contact information.
(D) Some payment details.

This is the end of the Listening test. Turn to Part 5 in your test book.

GO ON TO THE NEXT PAGE

READING TEST

In the Reading test, you will read a variety of texts and answer several different types of reading comprehension questions. The entire Reading test will last 75 minutes. There are three parts, and directions are given for each part. You are encouraged to answer as many questions as possible within the time allowed.

You must mark your answers on the separate answer sheet. Do not write your answers in your test book.

PART 5

Directions: A word or phrase is missing in each of the sentences below. Four answer choices are given below each sentence. Select the best answer to complete the sentence. Then mark the letter (A), (B), (C), or (D) on your answer sheet.

101. Simpson and Sons Landscaping has been ------- recommended by several neighboring businesses.
(A) high
(B) highly
(C) highest
(D) higher

102. Mrs. Watanabe wants to know when ------- shipment will be ready for delivery.
(A) her
(B) hers
(C) she
(D) herself

103. Due to the power outage, the marketing meeting has been rescheduled ------- tomorrow.
(A) at
(B) for
(C) in
(D) by

104. Trakstar's newest data collection algorithm makes it much ------- for business owners to generate mailing lists.
(A) easy
(B) easily
(C) easier
(D) easiest

105. By ------- retail locations in Beijing, Manila, and Kuala Lumpur, Carrington Ltd. has continued its growth into overseas markets.
(A) opens
(B) open
(C) opening
(D) opened

106. The ceramic tiles may be weakened ------- the kiln's heat is set too low.
(A) so
(B) if
(C) but
(D) why

107. Seven Miles High is the second ------- distributed in-flight magazine in the global airline industry.
(A) wide
(B) widen
(C) more widely
(D) most widely

108. Crazy Steve's Bar and Grill will be closed next weekend to accommodate a private -------.
(A) expense
(B) function
(C) customer
(D) occasion

109. Dr. Morgan Piersall, the keynote speaker at this year's National Fishing and Wildlife Expo, ------- several revolutionary depth location devices.
(A) enrolled
(B) communicated
(C) invented
(D) exceeded

110. During today's meeting, Ms. Robinson made a point of ------- the sales team for their exceptional results last month.
(A) congratulating
(B) congratulatory
(C) congratulation
(D) congratulate

111. The consumer satisfaction survey results are ------- to differ among age groups.
(A) likely
(B) probable
(C) recent
(D) important

112. Beginning October 31, the accounting department will issue sales commissions ------- from biweekly paychecks.
(A) separating
(B) separation
(C) separates
(D) separately

113. The course taught by Reed McIntyre is geared toward ------- students interested in computers or tech-related careers.
(A) which
(B) whose
(C) either
(D) those

114. Online debit card transactions are ------- in the user's account immediately.
(A) reflects
(B) reflecting
(C) reflect
(D) reflected

115. The new Fraud Alert program allows bank customers to ------- their account for any suspicious activity.
(A) monitored
(B) monitor
(C) monitoring
(D) monitors

116. Consult our press kit for facts and information ------- our company's colorful history.
(A) pending
(B) regarding
(C) within
(D) throughout

117. Please review the travel itinerary carefully ------- it has been received from the communications department.
(A) ever since
(B) as soon as
(C) then
(D) while

118. ------- of the service writer include detailed cost estimates and ensuring customer satisfaction.
(A) Productions
(B) Responsibilities
(C) Promotions
(D) Offerings

119. Our firm is dedicated to protecting the ------- of our clients' affairs.
(A) confiding
(B) confides
(C) confidential
(D) confidentiality

120. ------- an increase in affordable arc welders, metal sculpture has become a more accessible and popular art medium.
(A) Rather than
(B) Such as
(C) Due to
(D) Instead of

GO ON TO THE NEXT PAGE

121. Our investment in LED light bulbs played a key ------- in reducing our operating expenses by cutting down on electricity usage.
(A) basis
(B) agency
(C) factor
(D) role

122. The scheduled construction of a new subway station in Richland Village has created a ------- demand for skilled workers.
(A) sizable
(B) durable
(C) lengthy
(D) tidy

123. The spokesperson stated that the buy-out was successfully completed ------- third-party arbitration.
(A) thanks to
(B) even if
(C) as well as
(D) overall

124. The marketing team for Vedder Sporting Goods is ------- a branding campaign to target younger consumers.
(A) considers
(B) consider
(C) considered
(D) considering

125. Last year, Cooper-Staubach Industries ------- an internship program for engineering students studying industrial aviation.
(A) signaled
(B) established
(C) demonstrated
(D) specialized

126. ------- a brief slump in summer sales, the Smile Motor Company exceeded second quarter earnings expectations.
(A) In case
(B) Because
(C) In spite of
(D) Concerning

127. The plan to ------- the Sioux City processing facility will have a significant impact on Honeybee Farm's overall poultry productivity.
(A) expansion
(B) expanded
(C) expanse
(D) expand

128. ------- being the critic's least favorite film at the Venice Film Festival, *Addicted to Love* nevertheless won the People's Choice Award for best visual effects.
(A) Furthermore
(B) Without
(C) Despite
(D) Until

129. We found the Aloha Point-of-Sale (POS) solution to be the only system ------- for our needs.
(A) extensive
(B) adequate
(C) attractive
(D) deliberate

130. Mr. Gomez correctly predicted that sales would decrease ------- as the company scaled back on social media advertising.
(A) productively
(B) incrementally
(C) arguably
(D) reportedly

Directions: Read the texts that follow. A word, phrase, or sentence is missing in parts of the each text. Four answer choices are given below each of the text. Select the best answer to complete the text. Then mark the letter (A), (B), (C), or (D) on your answer sheet.

Questions 131-134 refer to the following article.

J.P. Esquire International to Acquire Constellation Technology

SEATTLE — J.P. Esquire International (JPEI) announced Wednesday that ------- would
131.
purchase Constellation Technology in a deal valued at $250 million.

A spokesperson for JPEI said the company expects to double its profits by the end of next year. It will accomplish this by making full use of Constellation's recently updated production facilities. -------.
132.

Financial experts believe the Constellation acquisition will make JPEI the world's leading producer of circuits. "They will be well ahead of their -------." said
133.
top analyst Vince Rizzo.

J.P. Esquire plans to maintain Constellation's current workforce, with each of Constellation's factories continuing normal operations for the next five years. -------, JPEI will evaluate whether
134.
additional staff are needed.

131. (A) it
(B) he
(C) those
(D) someone

132. (A) The transaction should improve morale
(B) All four are operating at maximum capacity
(C) Another company will be acquired next year
(D) Offers from other firms were rejected

133. (A) critics
(B) suppliers
(C) investors
(D) competitors

134. (A) As you requested
(B) As a matter of fact
(C) After all
(D) After that time

GO ON TO THE NEXT PAGE

Desert Oasis Inn: Reservations

We recommend reservations because hotel accommodations at the Desert Oasis Inn are very -------.
                        135.

Reservations will be held with a one-night deposit or 50 percent of total room charges for stays of longer than one night.

Cancellations made more than seven days prior to your scheduled arrival date ------- in full.
       136.

If, for some reason, a reservation must be cancelled within one week of your scheduled arrival date, charges for the entire ------- of your stay will be billed
                                             137.

to you. -------.
     138.

---

135. (A) limits
    (B) limited
    (C) limitation
    (D) limiting

136. (A) are refunding
    (B) had been refunding
    (C) will be refunded
    (D) were refunded

137. (A) area
    (B) height
    (C) length
    (D) sense

138. (A) This policy applies to early departure as well
    (B) In addition, we will soon open another store in Oasis
    (C) We hope that you have enjoyed your stay
    (D) Hotel guests are welcome to cancel at any time

Computer Funds Allocated

New technology is coming ------- the students of Arlington
                    139.

Heights. On Friday, Mayor Leland Morris announced

that his "The Future is Digital" proposal was approved

by the Board of Supervisors. -------. The program allots
                            140.

$150,000 to each school in the city for the purchase of

computers. Students will be allowed to take home

laptops and tablets ------- for special assignments and
                      141.

class projects, but they will normally ------- to the students
                        142.

only during school hours.

139. (A) to
    (B) at
    (C) from
    (D) on

140. (A) The desks will be purchased at a discount rate
    (B) The final decision is expected next month
    (C) Nevertheless, the mayor remains content with the decision
    (D) The vote took place on Wednesday, July 6

141. (A) occasionally
    (B) exceptionally
    (C) finally
    (D) supposedly

142. (A) are available
    (B) not available
    (C) be available
    (D) were availed

GO ON TO THE NEXT PAGE

December 2
Ms. Tracy Jordan
ASAP Travel Partners
4300 W. Armitage Avenue
Chicago, IL 60631

Dear Ms. Jordan,

Thank you for your purchase of 10 Fratello GN460 High-Yield Black Toner Cartridges from Office Oracle. Your online order was received on December 1 and is ready for shipping. ------- .
143.

We appreciate that you have chosen Office Oracle for your company's clerical and office needs. As a show of thanks, we are applying a 10 percent discount to this ------- order. ------- , we are
144.   **145.**
including a reimbursement of shipping charges. Enclosed you will find the adjusted invoice and a check for $17.50.

Office Oracle is pleased to welcome you to the family and ------- to
146.
providing you with quality products and service in the future.

Sincerely,
Udee Aritisi
Customer Service Representative
Enclosure

143. (A) Your interest in employment opportunities with us is appreciated
(B) Unfortunately, we are writing to inform you of a delay in delivery
(C) However, it seems that you have failed to reply
(D) You may expect to receive your order in 5-7 business days

144. (A) ongoing
(B) complimentary
(C) particular
(D) sequential

145. (A) For example
(B) Still
(C) However
(D) Additionally

146. (A) leaves room
(B) pushes harder
(C) goes back
(D) looks forward

Directions: In this part you will read a selection of texts, such as magazine and newspaper articles, e-mails, and instant messages. Each text or set of texts is followed by several questions. Select the best answer for each question and mark the letter (A), (B), (C), or (D) on your answer sheet.

Questions 147-148 refer to the following invoice.

UPTOWN THEATER

1001 Broadway Avenue
Easton

Invoice #: 0411-5662-UT*

*Keep this invoice number handy. You will need it if you have to contact customer service.

Received from Carl Culver: $199.98 payment to Uptown Theater, charged to credit card ending in xxxx-5622

Description: Tickets for Bill Derby Trio in concert Saturday, April 11. Doors at 7:30 P.M.

IMPORTANT: Please print this invoice and bring it with you to the venue. No paper invoice will be mailed. Be sure to arrive early to check your name on the preorder list at the ticket counter. Visit our website for our ticket refund policy.

---

147. What does Mr. Culver plan to do on April 11?
(A) Call the theater.
(B) Travel abroad.
(C) Pay his credit card bill.
(D) Attend a musical event.

148. What must Mr. Culver bring with him?
(A) A credit card.
(B) Paper tickets.
(C) A copy of an invoice.
(D) A form of identification.

GO ON TO THE NEXT PAGE

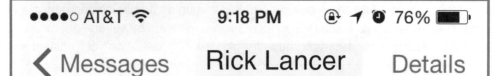

●●●●○ AT&T 📶   9:18 PM   ⊙ ✈ ⏱ 76% 🔋

< Messages   **Rick Lancer**   Details

Maria, I'm at the Armitage Hotel, installing the new sound system. Raphael called in sick, and this job is too complicated to do alone. It's not what I expected. It's a large space that can be divided into smaller rooms, and the hotel wants a programmable system to work when the space is used for more than one meeting or dinner scheduled at the same time. Can you get in touch with Gary Winters and ask him to come help me? I don't have his mobile phone number.

149. What problem does Mr. Lancer have?
(A) He is unable to do a job by himself.
(B) He feels sick and cannot work.
(C) He will not be able to attend a scheduled meeting.
(D) He does not know how to contact a vendor.

150. Why did Mr. Lancer send the text message to Maria?
(A) To have her reschedule a meeting at a hotel.
(B) To cancel an event in the hotel ballroom.
(C) To ask her to make a call.
(D) To request special equipment.

The Swank Oasis Hotel & Spa

CUSTOMER SATISFACTION SURVEY

Thank you for staying at the Swank Oasis Hotel & Spa. Customer satisfaction is very important to us, and we would appreciate your feedback. Please fill out the survey below and leave it with the receptionist at the front desk when you check out.

How satisfied were you with the Swank Oasis Hotel & Spa?
Please circle one selection for each category:

SERVICE	Not satisfied	Satisfied	**(Very Satisfied)**
CLEANLINESS	Not satisfied	Satisfied	**(Very Satisfied)**
APPEARANCE	Not satisfied	Satisfied	**(Very Satisfied)**
RESTAURANT	Not satisfied	**(Satisfied)**	Very Satisfied

Would you recommend the Swank Oasis Hotel & Spa to others?

	No	Maybe	**(Yes)**

Please add any comments or suggestions you may have in the space below:

All in all, I had a highly satisfactory experience at the Hotel & Spa. The hotel employees were extremely friendly. The spa was very clean and comfortable. Thanks to the well-equipped facilities, I was able to enjoy a relaxing stay. The restaurant, however, though inexpensive, was not particularly memorable.

If you wish to be contacted with promotional offers, please provide your name and phone number or e-mail address.

Steve Bruges	s_bruges@ivria.com

151. What are guests asked to do?
  (A) Tell their friends about the hotel.
  (B) Recommend staff members for awards.
  (C) Return a completed form.
  (D) Leave their keys at the front desk.

152. What is suggested about Mr. Bruges?
  (A) He is an experienced masseuse.
  (B) He would like a job in the hotel industry.
  (C) He would stay at the hotel again.
  (D) He would like to discuss his stay with hotel staff.

GO ON TO THE NEXT PAGE

Questions 153-154 refer to the following online chat discussion.

Linda Chevalier 4:04 P.M.

I've never participated in a training session online. I just go to the website address you e-mailed me, and click the Join button, right?

Gus LaMotta 4:02 P.M.

Correct. Then you'll need to enter the access code: AXCORP.

Linda Chevalier 4:04 P.M.

A pop-up window gave me this message. "Error Code: 404. Access Denied." Is that the right code?

Gus LaMotta 4:05 P.M.

Let me double-check. Might be a mistake.

Linda Chevalier 4:05 P.M.

Or maybe there's an issue with the website?

Gus LaMotta 4:06 P.M.

Yeah. My bad. I gave you the meeting code instead of the access code. Try EVANSTON.

Linda Chevalier 4:07 P.M.

Bingo! Thanks.

Gus LaMotta 4:08 P.M.

Great. Make sure your audio is on. Click the ENABLE WEB CAM button at the top right of the screen. You'll see and hear the trainer, and vice versa. To eliminate background noise, you may want to mute your microphone until prompted to speak.

153. At 4:06 P.M., what does Mr. LaMotta most likely mean when he writes, "My bad"?
   (A) The training has been accomplished.
   (B) The Web site is unavailable.
   (C) He made a mistake.
   (D) He thought of something else.

154. What is probably true about Mr. LaMotta?
   (A) He has recently received a new computer.
   (B) He does not have permission to attend the meeting.
   (C) He often participates in conference calls.
   (D) He is familiar with the training session.

Duggar Elite Systems, LLC 1301 Punchbowl St, Honolulu, HI 96813, USA	
Invoice: DES-982354	Shipped on: June 19

Billed to:	Dr. Virgil Spires Straub Medical Center Hawaii Pacific University Hospital 888 S King St, Honolulu, HI 96810, USA

Item Code	Description	Quantity
6SNUGS4	Polyurethane Dressing	15
3HSINM3***	Tracheotomy Barrier Shield	25
2NONDM7	Drain Sponge (50 ct.)	10
9DDOCK0	Surgical Gloves (100 ct.)	60

***Item 3HSINM3 will be delivered at a later date because they are currently not in the warehouse.

155. What most likely is Duggar Elite Systems?
(A) A clothing manufacturer.
(B) A medical supply company.
(C) A hospital.
(D) A doctor's office.

156. According to the invoice, what happened on June 19?
(A) A payment was refunded.
(B) A shipment was delivered.
(C) An invoice was revised.
(D) An order was shipped.

157. What is indicated about the barrier shields?
(A) They are out of stock at the moment.
(B) They are available in one color only.
(C) They are no longer manufactured.
(D) They are the wrong size.

GO ON TO THE NEXT PAGE.

To: All Staff
From: Jeffrey Perlman
Re: Office Expenses
Date: Monday, October 3

We've all seen the expense report from last quarter, and it is clear that we need to reduce our costs on office supplies.

So, it's pretty obvious that we can start saving immediately on printing and copying documents.

Not to point any fingers, but a number of us have been making color copies of general documents, such as travel itineraries, prototype drafts, and deadline schedules. ---[1]---

Purchasing frequent replacements inevitably leaves us with less money to spend on things like business travel and social events. ---[2]---

While we could implement a system wherein all jobs must first be approved by the department supervisors, I would prefer that employees make their own decisions about printing and copying. ---[3]---

Please reserve the use of color for only those cases where visual appeal is a significant factor. Publicity flyers intended for clients are one obvious example. ---[4]---

Thank you for your attention to this matter.

158. What is one purpose of the memo?
(A) To inform a staff of an error in a document.
(B) To request cooperation with a departmental procedure.
(C) To delay the release of a quarterly expense report.
(D) To alert employees to a budget concern.

159. What are employees advised to do?
(A) Distribute travel itineraries by e-mail.
(B) Get prior approval from their supervisors.
(C) Make black and white copies of basic documents.
(D) Tell co-workers about upcoming social events.

160. In which of the positions marked [1], [2], [3], and [4] does the following sentence best belong?
"While multicolor documents are more attractive and eye-pleasing than black-and-white, color ink cartridges are pricy and inefficient."
(A) [1].
(B) [2].
(C) [3].
(D) [4].

Recycling Survey in Progress

Many St. Claire residents, businesses and visitors have expressed concerns to town officials about inadequate recycling facilities. ---[1]---

With a data-collection project scheduled to begin on Tuesday, led by Moogley Associates of St. Claire, town officials will soon learn the extent of the recycling output on a typical weekday, during the evening, and at peak times when events are taking place in town. ---[2]--- When it is completed, the study will provide updated statistics of all public and private recyclable material produced in the area and typical rates of disposal.

---[3]--- "The general consensus is that the demand has increased with the four businesses and the two residential developments we've seen in the last five years," said Planning Director Maria Stotts. "But we need hard data before we can consider another costly recycling facility."

---[4]---

161. How many recycling centers are currently in St. Claire?
(A) one
(B) two
(C) four
(D) five

162. In which of the positions marked [1], [2], [3], and [4] does the following sentence best belong?
"Some have called for construction of a second recycling center in the next two years."
(A) [1].
(B) [2].
(C) [3].
(D) [4].

163. What does the article indicate about the survey?
(A) It will study the demand for recycling in three local neighborhoods.
(B) It will measure the demand for recycling at various times.
(C) It will be paid for by Moogley Associates of St. Claire.
(D) It will be conducted by St. Claire's planning director.

GO ON TO THE NEXT PAGE

Start-Up Guru Coming to Laramie

LARAMIE (March 9) - Evan Smith, dubbed the "Bill Gates of startups" by the *Wyoming Tribune Eagle*, will be the keynote speaker at the 12th annual Laramie Small Business Expo (LSBE). The Expo will take place at the Wyoming Civic Center from April 13 to April 16. More than 1,000 start-up entrepreneurs will attend workshops and showcase their businesses at booths, where visitors can examine products and ask questions.

According to an LSBE press release, Mr. Smith will feature many of the ideas from his bestselling book "The Art of the Startup" published just last year. Mr. Smith believes that there are several key decisions that must be made before launching any new business scheme. "You can't be starting from the idea of creating a product you want to sell," Mr. Smith writes in his book.

"The golden rule is to create a product people want to buy. And it is unquestionably crucial to get this right if you want your business to succeed."

Mr. Smith is the owner of several successful businesses in Portland, where he has lived for the past decade. "I was born and raised in Laramie," Mr. Smith said. "So I wanted to give back to the community where I got my start in any way I could, which is why I accepted the invitation to participate in the Expo. There's an outstanding opportunity there for start-up entrepreneurs. Following the simple but ultimately effective guidelines in my book worked well for me and for many other successful start-ups." Admission to the Expo is $20 per day, but tickets can be purchased for $15 in advance through LSBE's website at: www.lsbe.com/expo.

164. What is the article mainly about?
(A) A business figure's participation in an event.
(B) The drawbacks of running a small business.
(C) The opening of a start-up.
(D) New trends in marketing.

165. Why did Mr. Smith decide to participate in the Expo?
(A) He wants to support entrepreneurs in his hometown.
(B) He is doing research for a new training seminar.
(C) He would like to recruit some investors.
(D) He is looking for ways to increase production.

166. What does Mr. Smith say is the most important consideration for new entrepreneurs?
(A) Manufacturing a product in a cost-effective way.
(B) Creating a product that the business owner feels passionate about.
(C) Marketing a product on social media.
(D) Developing a product that is desired by consumers.

167. According to the article, what has Mr. Smith recently done?
(A) He survived a major accident.
(B) He traveled to Laramie.
(C) He wrote a book.
(D) He presented an award.

Your Opinion Is Important to Us

The Grayson Corporation has been conducting public opinion polls on current affairs since 1974.

All our polls are based on telephone interviews with adults 18 years of age or older who live in specific polling regions. To ensure that every adult living within a polling area has an equal chance of being contacted, potential interviewees are selected by a computer algorithm that generates phone numbers from all telecom networks.

To find out what people think about what is happening in the world these days, visit our Hot List page. New polls are published weekly, and all polls are stored and accessible online. If you prefer to search for polls by subject, go to our A-Z Directory page. If you would like to reproduce tables, charts, or any other graphics created by Grayson, go to the **Contact Us** page and click the link for our Licensing Division. There you will find an easy-to-use online form to fill out with details about how and where you intend to use the information. In most cases, a response is provided within 24 hours of submission.

168. In paragraph1, line 2 the word "affairs" is closest in meaning to
(A) proposals.
(B) contracts.
(C) relationships.
(D) issues.

169. What is NOT mentioned about poll participants?
(A) They are interviewed over the phone.
(B) They are adults.
(C) They are randomly selected.
(D) They are interviewed in groups.

170. What is indicated about the Grayson Corporation?
(A) It is searching for new markets.
(B) It publishes telephone directories.
(C) It updates its website every week.
(D) It has offices in multiple locations.

171. How can readers get permission to reproduce graphics?
(A) By submitting a paper form.
(B) By providing information online.
(C) By visiting a retail location.
(D) By making a phone call.

GO ON TO THE NEXT PAGE.

Vincent Ellerbosch [5:52 P.M.]

Hi, everyone. I just got in the conference room, and I am having some trouble with the projector. It keeps shutting off. Does anyone know why?

Onat Cheetslong [5:55 P.M.]

This happened to me last time. Try pushing the gray reset button.

Natalie Goff [5:55 P.M.]

Wasn't everything supposed to be set up by 3:30 this afternoon? I hope we'll be able to get everything ready before the board members start arriving.

Vincent Ellerbosch [5:58 P.M.]

Glynn Davis was supposed to do it, but there was another meeting in the room and it ran late. She couldn't wait, so she asked me to set up once the room was free.

Vincent Ellerbosch [5:59 P.M.]

No, it doesn't work. Onat, can you come down here?

Onat Cheetslong [5:50 P.M.]

On my way.

Natalie Goff [5:51 P.M.]

Are you all set otherwise?

Vincent Ellerbosch [5:52 P.M.]

Yes, Natalie, everything is ready for the presentations. I ran them by a few colleagues to make sure that everything is clear. I've made hard copies of the presentation and the report which the board members will receive.

Natalie Goff [5:55 P.M.]

Good. I will be there at 8:00 P.M. sharp to take everyone to dinner and then to their respective hotels. I will distribute the reports then too, so please make sure that they are completed before then. I will bring the group back tomorrow morning at 9:30 for the demo and closing sessions.

Vincent Ellerbosch [5:59 P.M.]

Thanks. The projector is working fine now. Onat attached a different power cord.

172. What is Mr. Ellerbosch trying to do?
(A) Train new employees.
(B) Meet with Ms. Goff.
(C) Copy some documents.
(D) Prepare a room for a meeting.

173. Why was the conference room not set up by 3:30 P.M.?
(A) Because Ms. Davis was not at work.
(B) Because the new employees arrived late.
(C) Because the projector had not been located.
(D) Because a meeting did not end on time.

174. At 5:50 P.M., what does Mr. Cheetslong most likely mean when he writes, "On my way"?
(A) He is greeting some board members.
(B) He will meet Ms. Goff at the hotel.
(C) He will finish reviewing some slides.
(D) He is coming to help Mr. Ellerbosch.

175. What will happen at 8:00 P.M.?
(A) Board members will listen to a presentation.
(B) Board members will return from the security office.
(C) Ms. Goff will go to the conference room.
(D) Mr. Ellerbosch will complete some forms.

GO ON TO THE NEXT PAGE.

Wendy Jurassic
928 East Avon Avenue
Woodland Hills, MI 58902

May 20

Dear Ms. Jurassic,

We sincerely appreciate you coming in to interview for the senior Web administrator position at Forkel & Associates. However, I regret to inform you that the personnel department decided to go with another candidate. Nevertheless, we were impressed by the knowledge and experience that you displayed during your interview and have decided to offer you another recently-vacated position.

In contrast to the position you applied for, this position is part-time. You would be working on Tuesday, Wednesday, and Friday from 1 to 5 PM and on Monday and Thursday from 2 to 6 PM. Your responsibilities would include maintaining domain security, updating server patches, analyzing Web logs, and developing a content management system.

If you are interested in this position, please call me at 555-0923 or e-mail me at k_neierbaum@forkel.com.

Sincerely,
Kurtz Neierbaum

From:	Wendy Jurassic <r_jurassic@inmail.com>
To:	Kurtz Neierbaum <k_neierbaum@forkel.com>
Re:	Part-time opportunity
Date:	May 23

Dear Mr. Neierbaum

I'm writing with regard to your letter of May 20. It's unfortunate that the position I applied for has been filled, but I would be very pleased to accept the new position that you are offering. However, I was wondering if you would be agreeable to a minor change regarding the hours I would be working.

During my interview, I referenced my experience volunteering with World Vision. I was recently offered a position working part-time for them, but there is a schedule conflict. I work for them Tuesday, Wednesday, and Thursday from 9 AM to 1 PM. Would it be possible for me to work for you from 1:30 to 5:30 PM on Tuesday and Wednesday? If so, please let me know at your earliest convenience.

Incidentally, the duties that I currently perform for World Vision are exactly the same as the responsibilities of the position with Forkel & Associates. So, I believe that I would adjust very quickly to working for Forkel.

I look forward to becoming a valuable member of Forkel & Associates.

Sincerely,
Wendy Jurassic

GO ON TO THE NEXT PAGE

176. For what type of position did Ms. Jurassic apply for?
    (A) Legal assistance.
    (B) Graphic design.
    (C) Accounting.
    (D) Information technology.

177. In the letter, the phrase "In contrast to" in paragraph 2, line 1 is closest on meaning to
    (A) supporting.
    (B) against.
    (C) identical.
    (D) unlike.

178. What is suggested about Forkel & Associates?
    (A) It has opened a new retail location.
    (B) It opens at 1 P.M. on certain days of the week.
    (C) It has signed several new clients.
    (D) It recently hired a full-time employee.

179. Why was the e-mail written?
    (A) To recommend someone for a position.
    (B) To clarify information about a volunteer opportunity.
    (C) To request an adjustment to a job schedule.
    (D) To negotiate the salary being offered for a job.

180. What most likely is NOT a task Ms. Jurassic does at World Vision?
    (A) Update the server.
    (B) Manage content.
    (C) File tax forms.
    (D) Analyze Web logs.

Employee Report for Annual Performance Review

DuPont Museum of Natural History
Conservation and Collections Department

Name: Dana Mayberry

Title: Associate Scientist II

Please list all major projects in which you participated this year:

1. Conducted two-week course in archaeological site preservation for university students majoring in Paleontology. (Feb 5-Feb 19)

2. Represented Department of Conservation and Collections at Archaeological Institute of America (AIA) annual Conference on Natural History, Albany, NY. (March 20-March 24)

3. Presented paper, "Building a Strong Future for Archaeological Outreach and Education", at the AIA 2-day working conference in New Orleans, LA. (May 22-23)

4. Conducted research on illicit antiquities found in major national collections. (April-Sept) Article was submitted to Journal of World Archaeology and accepted for publication.

5. Led tours on weekends during opening celebration of new Dinosaur exhibition. (Nov 1-Nov 30)

GO ON TO THE NEXT PAGE.

Dana Mayberry of Evanston Receives Award

— Yale T. Briggs, Local News Reporter

[CHICAGO] January 23 — Evanston native Dana Mayberry has received the Hope Lawler Award from the Archaeological Institute of America for her research on archaeological education. She works at the DuPont Museum of Natural History as an associate scientist.

Davidson Perry-Watts, director of the DuPont Museum, said that it is very rare for the award to be given to a scientist so early in her career. It is a tribute to Dana's dedication and hard work, said Mr. Perry-Watts. "We are very happy to have her on our team."

Ms. Mayberry began work as a researcher after receiving a Master's degree in museum studies at Iowa State University. She is a graduate of Lake Forest High School.

The award will be presented on March 18 at the annual AIA Conference on Natural History, this year held in Las Vegas, NV.

181. According to the report, why did Ms. Mayberry go to New Orleans?
(A) To enter a new course of study.
(B) To begin a new job.
(C) To give a talk based on her research.
(D) To make a sales presentation.

182. What does the report suggest happened at DuPont Museum in November?
(A) A conference was held.
(B) A multimedia system was finally replaced.
(C) A new exhibition was opened.
(D) A research project was conducted.

183. Where did the article most likely appear?
(A) In a promotional booklet.
(B) In a museum brochure.
(C) In a scientific journal.
(D) In a town newspaper.

184. What does the article imply about the Hope Lawler Award?
(A) It is funded by taxpayers.
(B) It is usually presented to a senior researcher.
(C) It is the highest honor in the DuPont.
(D) It is only awarded once per decade.

185. What is suggested about the Conference on Natural History?
(A) It is one of several held by the AIA.
(B) It is open to the public.
(C) It is free for university researchers.
(D) It is held in a different location each year.

Monday, June 23

Levinson Financial Offices to Be Relocated

NEW YORK—Levinson Financial of New York State will soon be moving its personnel in Rochester, Syracuse, and Buffalo into company-owned buildings. The high cost of leasing office space <u>prompted</u> the company's decision to build. "After renting for ten years, we realized that ownership would result in significant savings," said Jamie Frazier, Levinson Financial managing director. She also noted that sharing space with other firms had become increasingly untenable. Construction of the Rochester facility, which began a year ago, was finished earlier this month. Employees will likely move in as soon as August.

Construction of the other two facilities, in Syracuse and Buffalo, began in February and is expected to wrap up within the next few months. The company says that its entire staff will relocate to one of the new buildings by November at the latest.

GO ON TO THE NEXT PAGE

Aladdin
Transfer & Storage

HOME   MOVING SERVICES   RESOURCE CENTER   ABOUT   TESTIMONIALS   CONTACT

Aladdin makes moving easier from start to finish!

We are honest about costs. A relocation consultant will visit your site to complete a visual survey of the items to be moved. We will provide a written estimate within 2 days of the visit. We work with you throughout the move.

- Do you need help packaging? Our crew will assist you with anything from furniture to computer systems and general equipment.

- Are you moving sensitive documents and files? With your security staff, we can create a schedule to ensure continuous monitoring of confidential material.

- Do you need **storage** space? We can hold your belongings at our secure, climate-controlled warehouse until your new space is ready.

We get the job done right. The move isn't finished until every crate is unpacked, every item placed, every piece of debris discarded.

Please complete the request below to schedule an on-site cost estimate.	
Company name:	Levinson Financial NY
Name of contact person:	Lane Rowley
Telephone:	210-888-4343
E-mail:	land_d@levinson.com
Pick-up address:	128 Forbes Lane, Rochester
Delivery address:	548 Village Gate Road, Rochester
Pick-up date:	August 10
Delivery date:	August 10
Preferred visual survey date and time:	August 1, between 9:00 AM and 5:00 PM

186. In the article, paragraph 1, line 5, the word "prompted" is the closest in meaning to
(A) initiated.
(B) acted quickly.
(C) made different.
(D) reminded.

187. What is implied about Ms. Frazier?
(A) She works in the Levinson Financial Syracuse office.
(B) She was promoted to managing director last year.
(C) She has been employed by Levinson Financial for 10 years.
(D) She will move to a new office by November.

188. What service does Aladdin offer?
(A) Building construction.
(B) Corporate catering.
(C) Transfer of sensitive material.
(D) Management of computer systems.

189. What is implied about the Village Gate Road Location?
(A) It was constructed in about one year.
(B) It has recently been vacated.
(C) It is partially leased to other companies.
(D) It will hold 500 employees.

190. What will most likely happen on August 1?
(A) Mr. Rowley will receive a written estimate.
(B) Furniture crates will be unpacked.
(C) Equipment will be removed from storage.
(D) An Aladdin employee will visit the Forbes Lane location.

GO ON TO THE NEXT PAGE.

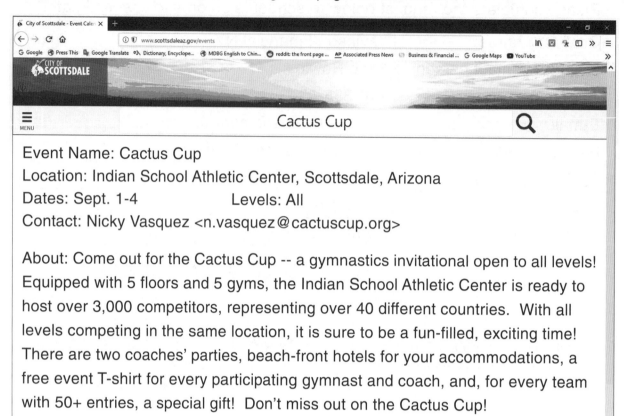

Event Name: Cactus Cup
Location: Indian School Athletic Center, Scottsdale, Arizona
Dates: Sept. 1-4   Levels: All
Contact: Nicky Vasquez <n.vasquez@cactuscup.org>

About: Come out for the Cactus Cup -- a gymnastics invitational open to all levels! Equipped with 5 floors and 5 gyms, the Indian School Athletic Center is ready to host over 3,000 competitors, representing over 40 different countries. With all levels competing in the same location, it is sure to be a fun-filled, exciting time! There are two coaches' parties, beach-front hotels for your accommodations, a free event T-shirt for every participating gymnast and coach, and, for every team with 50+ entries, a special gift! Don't miss out on the Cactus Cup!

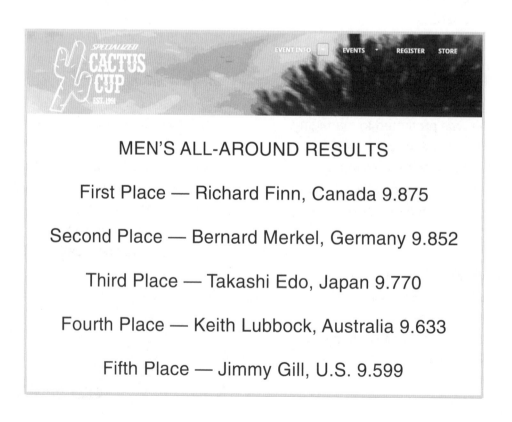

MEN'S ALL-AROUND RESULTS

First Place — Richard Finn, Canada 9.875

Second Place — Bernard Merkel, Germany 9.852

Third Place — Takashi Edo, Japan 9.770

Fourth Place — Keith Lubbock, Australia 9.633

Fifth Place — Jimmy Gill, U.S. 9.599

What's new in Scottsdale?

The annual Cactus Cup Gymnastics Invitational took place last weekend and it was a blockbuster success! Because of the participation of elite competitors, the number of visitors was double that of previous years.

The contest <u>drew</u> athletes for both the solo and team categories. G-Force Acrobatic of San Diego, California, won its third straight team title. All of the events were highly competitive, featuring wonderful feats of athleticism, but by far the most exciting event was the Men's All-Around.

Richard Finn from Canada beat two-time champion Bernard Merkel from Germany with two perfect 10 scores on the high bar and rings, respectively. All the athletes were amazing but my personal favorite was Takashi Edo, a Japanese phenomenon on the parallel bars. His double-backward somersault dismount was something no one had ever seen before.

Spectators could join the fun, too. Gymnasts who were not competing led a community course on floor exercise. This, along with music and vendors, provided the perfect way to enjoy the last weekend of the summer.

By Dwayne Mustaine

---

191. What is indicated about contestants?
(A) They are all amateurs.
(B) They are from a variety of countries.
(C) They are acquainted with Ms. Vasquez.
(D) They are requested to register in advance.

192. What is indicated about this year's event?
(A) It was held in Scottsdale for the first time.
(B) It was better attended than last year's event.
(C) It had more than 10,000 visitors.
(D) It cost $5 per person to attend.

193. In the article, the word "drew" in the paragraph 2, line 1, is closest in meaning to
(A) moved.
(B) attracted.
(C) won.
(D) pictured.

194. What is stated about Mr. Merkel?
(A) He fell on a dismount.
(B) He recently moved to Canada.
(C) He won the competition previously.
(D) He has given gymnastics lessons.

195. Whose performance did Mr. Mustaine like the most?
(A) Finn's.
(B) Edo's.
(C) Lubbock's.
(D) Gill's.

GO ON TO THE NEXT PAGE.

Soho Hotels Get New Owner

DES MOINES (July) — The London-based Staybridge Hotel Group has acquired Soho, Inc., a small but exclusive locally franchised hotel chain. With the addition of the Soho properties, Staybridge now operates 11 hotels in the Des Moines area with more than 800 guest rooms.

Prior to the acquisition, Staybridge had been best known for its Staybridge Regency Suites, smaller hotels designed with business travelers in mind. Soho's four properties include the luxurious Lancaster, built in 1903, and The Grand Court, a high-end hotel that opened just last year.

The Soho hotels are a very welcome addition to the Staybridge Brand, said Staybridge spokesperson Blake Tyler. Soho has a solid reputation in Des Moines, and with accommodations that appeal especially to tourists, they are a perfect complement to Staybridge's existing hotels.

Staybridge loyalty-club members can now earn points when they stay at any of the former Soho Hotels.

Welcome to Des Moines! Want to be in the heart of the city center? Choose Staybridge Hotel Group. Our hotel family now includes the popular Soho Hotels. Below are a few of our most popular hotels in the downtown area.

The Lancaster — Featuring complimentary wireless Internet service, deluxe bed, large screen TVs and an indoor swimming pool, this hotel is located in one of the Twin Cities most historic buildings!

The Grand Court — Grand does not begin to describe this hotel! Enjoy our newly refurbished luxurious guest rooms, fine dining at our recently remodeled restaurant, and convenient access to theaters, shopping and sightseeing.

Hotel Hennepin — With free transportation to the airport and a fully equipped business center, this is the perfect hotel for working while traveling. Featuring conference rooms and complimentary wireless Internet service, this hotel makes it easy for business travelers.

Bankside Des Moines — An old-fashioned inn with modern conveniences such as microwaves, flat-screen TVs, and refrigerators in every room. With its charming decor, tasty complimentary breakfast, and proximity to sightseeing destinations, this is a wonderful place to stay during your Des Moines holiday.

Or choose one of our many other hotels in the Des Moines region. When you choose Staybridge, you choose the best!

GO ON TO THE NEXT PAGE.

Tripguru hotel ratings for Bankside Des Moines

Overall rating: 🎯 ◉◉◉◉○ Based on **534** traveller reviews

Most recent traveller reviews:

Cheskya Robelsk

Kiev, Ukraine

Overall Rating
◉◉◉○○

My recent stay at the Bankside was decent. My room was comfortable and well furnished, and all my meals at the hotel restaurant were tasty and not overpriced. The hotel staff provided adequate service as well. However, I wish there had been an airport shuttle service. I had a difficult time getting a taxi, and it was expensive. Aside from that minor inconvenience, I enjoyed my stay. Three out of five stars.

See rooms & rates

196. What does the article suggest about Staybridge Hotel Chains?
(A) It specializes in budget hotels.
(B) It wants to appeal to a wider variety of customers.
(C) It is relocating its headquarters.
(D) It has discontinued its rewards program.

197. What is indicated about the four hotels mentioned in the advertisement?
(A) They have business centers.
(B) They were first built in 1920.
(C) They are located in downtown Des Moines.
(D) They offer discounts to business travelers.

198. Which hotel is most likely not a Soho Property?
(A) The Lancaster.
(B) The Grand Court.
(C) Hotel Hennepin.
(D) Bankside Des Moines.

199. What information is provided about the hotel in which Ms. Robelsk has stayed?
(A) Its restaurant has been updated.
(B) It provides free breakfast.
(C) It is available for conferences.
(D) It includes a gift shop.

200. What disappointed Ms. Robelsk about her stay?
(A) The low quality of the restaurant.
(B) The lack of affordable transportation.
(C) The unfriendly staff.
(D) The high price of the room.

Stop! This is the end of the test. If you finish before time is called, you may go back to Parts 5, 6, and 7 and check your work.

New TOEIC Listening Script

PART 1

1. (   ) (A) The man is moving some boxes in a warehouse.
   (B) The man is installing a window in a factory.
   (C) The man is reading a newspaper in an airport.
   (D) The man is watching a movie in a theater.

2. (   ) (A) The worker is driving a truck.
   (B) The beach is full of trash.
   (C) The shovel is on the shelf.
   (D) The helmet is on the grass.

3. (   ) (A) The lawyer is taking some notes.
   (B) The doctor is giving the man a shot.
   (C) The chef is greeting a customer.
   (D) The teacher is erasing the blackboard.

4. (   ) (A) The man is using a computer.
   (B) The man is looking in a file cabinet.
   (C) The man is opening a door.
   (D) The man is sitting on the floor.

5. (   ) (A) Some people are working in a kitchen.
   (B) Some people are working in a bank.
   (C) Some people are watching a demonstration.
   (D) Some people are participating in a survey.

6. (   ) (A) Some people are shopping in the market.
   (B) Some people are lined up at an airport.
   (C) Some people are boarding a bus.
   (D) Some people are waiting for a train.

GO ON TO THE NEXT PAGE

PART 2

7. (   ) What time is the building inspector supposed to be here?
    (A) Sometime in the afternoon.
    (B) Yes, but they usually do.
    (C) The new subway station.

8. (   ) Excuse me, I'm looking for Gina's Hot Sauce.
    (A) That item is out of stock.
    (B) No, thanks.
    (C) I don't think she's here.

9. (   ) The warehouse is open, isn't it?
    (A) There should be plenty of room.
    (B) Mostly boxes of old files.
    (C) Yes, but I'm just about to lock it up.

10. (   ) When will the new line of products be released?
    (A) Most likely in late October.
    (B) Yes, an updated version.
    (C) It's one of my favorite cities.

11. (   ) Where is the nearest post office?
    (A) No, you didn't get any messages.
    (B) Couldn't tell you. I'm not from around here.
    (C) During my break.

12. (   ) Would you mind holding your meeting in conference room B tomorrow?
    (A) I thought he retired last year.
    (B) Sure, that works for me.
    (C) Yes, they're new workers.

13. (   ) How long will the interns work in the office?
    (A) Dave and Steve.
    (B) Only an hour or two.
    (C) You're welcome.

14. (   ) Isn't your driver's license due to expire this month?
    (A) She's an experienced driver.
    (B) It was much longer than that.
    (C) Oh, thanks for reminding me.

15. (   ) Should we be seated in a circle or set up in rows?
   (A) Aren't we going to be watching a video?
   (B) Just some coffee, please.
   (C) No. Arrange them according to size.

16. (   ) Why don't you try re-installing the software?
   (A) Depends on when the manager arrives.
   (B) That's the number for technical support.
   (C) I already tried that.

17. (   ) I don't recommend parking in the underground garage.
   (A) On the top shelf in the supply closet.
   (B) I've heard that before.
   (C) 50 copies, stapled please.

18. (   ) The trip shouldn't take longer than 20 minutes, should it?
   (A) No. It should be fairly quick.
   (B) Yes, it was quite informative.
   (C) No, you can walk there.

19. (   ) How can I reserve seats for the premiere of the film?
   (A) Right. That was yesterday.
   (B) Go to our website.
   (C) It went very well.

20. (   ) Have those property listings been updated yet?
   (A) I'll have some, thanks.
   (B) They're actually undersized.
   (C) We finished doing that before lunch.

21. (   ) Do you think Ms. Brown will give us more time on the budget reports?
   (A) The deadline is non-negotiable.
   (B) That makes it easier to make a decision.
   (C) Some took a bit longer.

22. (   ) Do you have any recommendations for Italian food?
   (A) I received her supervisor's approval.
   (B) Giuseppe's on Elm Street is fantastic.
   (C) A four-mile run.

GO ON TO THE NEXT PAGE.

23. (　) Please fill out this questionnaire before tomorrow's final interview.
    (A) I'll be sure to do that.
    (B) It's a new survey.
    (C) I saw him on the subway.

24. (　) Mr. Levin usually leaves the office at 5:30, doesn't he?
    (A) Five nights a week.
    (B) No. I ordered the fish.
    (C) Traffic was surprisingly light today.

25. (　) Where did the board of directors decide to build a new office tower?
    (A) Sales were average.
    (B) In Chicago.
    (C) October 1st.

26. (　) We're choosing new paint colors for the reception area.
    (A) Where's the waiter?
    (B) A new director was selected.
    (C) Coleman's Home & Hardware has a great selection.

27. (　) Why are these instructions only in Chinese?
    (A) Thanks for coming in early today.
    (B) I've asked Jill to have them translated.
    (C) We have enough copies for everyone.

28. (　) Which event space would you like to use?
    (A) Let's try for mid September.
    (B) We should hire her.
    (C) I like the first one you showed me.

29. (　) Who's recording the radio advertisement scripts?
    (A) We're open 24 hours.
    (B) At 7 o'clock on Monday.
    (C) That decision hasn't been made.

30. (　) Have you sent out the invitations for the grand opening?
    (A) I didn't get a guest list.
    (B) I'm planning on going too.
    (C) Outside of the conference center.

31. (　　) When will the car come to take us to the conference?
      (A) In front of the hotel.
      (B) The driver will call when he's arrived.
      (C) Because it's too far to walk.

PART 3

Questions 32 through 34 _refer to the following conversation._

W : Chad, what's going on with the special order of T-shirts for the San Diego Marathon? The event organizers are coming to pick them up this afternoon.

M : Had a bit of a setback, Lois. When I turned on the screen printing press this morning, I noticed the automatic squeegee had not been cleaned properly. So I had to take it apart and clean it before moving forward.

W : Oh, who was the last person to use the press?

M : I don't know. But I took care of it. No big deal. Cost me an hour, but I'll have the T-shirts ready this afternoon.

32. (　　) Where do the speakers most likely work?
      (A) At a custom print shop.
      (B) At a construction site.
      (C) In a bakery.
      (D) In an appliance store.

33. (　　) What problem does the man mention?
      (A) A shipment was delayed.
      (B) An order was cancelled.
      (C) An employee was late to work.
      (D) A machine was not cleaned properly.

34. (　　) What will happen this afternoon?
      (A) A business will close.
      (B) An order will be completed.
      (C) A repair person will arrive.
      (D) An event will be set up.

Questions 35 through 37 _refer to the following conversation._

M : Hey, I was here for the Tigers game, but I spent all my cash on snacks and drinks and souvenirs. Do you accept credit cards?

GO ON TO THE NEXT PAGE.

W : I can't process a credit card here at the exit, but you have two options. There's an ATM on the third level of the parking garage, right as you exit the concourse of the stadium. Or...if you have Internet access on your phone, you can pay online.

M : That's a great idea. I'll pay online. And, what's the website address that I should use?
W : The address is printed on the back of your parking ticket.

M : And then what?
W : Once you've paid the fee online, you'll get a confirmation code emailed to you. Give me the code and I'll process your exit.

35. (   ) Where are the speakers?
      (A) In a parking garage.
      (B) In a restaurant.
      (C) In a movie theater.
      (D) In a bank.

36. (   ) What does the man decide to do?
      (A) Withdraw money from a cash machine.
      (B) Call a customer service number.
      (C) Make a payment online.
      (D) Return at a later time.

37. (   ) What will be sent to the man?
      (A) A confirmation number.
      (B) A warranty offer.
      (C) An account statement.
      (D) A VIP membership card.

Questions 38 through 40 _refer to the following conversation._

M : Tiffany, you're coordinating the orientation program for new hires, correct? I need to double-check with you about the new sales associate. You still want me to review the benefits package with him, right?
W : I do. He'll be starting on Wednesday morning, and I was hoping you could talk to him right after lunch that afternoon.

M : Mmm... That's what I thought. I scheduled another meeting with Serena on Wednesday at 1 P.M. Is there any way that I can meet with the new guy in the morning?
W : Well, he's going to be working the floor in housewares, and they generally have a tight schedule for new hires. Don't worry about it. I'll have Jeff cover for you.

M : Thanks, Tiffany. Sorry about that.

38. (　　) What is the woman coordinating?
  (A) A company outing.
  (B) A grand opening.
  (C) A new employee orientation.
  (D) An annual performance review.

39. (　　) Where do the speakers most likely work?
  (A) At a travel agency.
  (B) At a department store.
  (C) At business school.
  (D) At a bank.

40. (　　) What does the woman say she will do?
  (A) Book a venue.
  (B) Prepare a contract.
  (C) Find a substitute.
  (D) Cancel an order.

Questions 41 through 43 *refer to the following conversation.*

M : Hello, I'd like two tickets to tonight's premiere of Titans of the Universe. I've heard it's an incredible film.

W : I'm sorry. The premiere has been sold out of tickets since last week. We still have some available for screenings tomorrow, though.

M : Oh, I kind of figured that would be the case. Tomorrow afternoon would work for us. Can I buy advance tickets?

W : We do offer advance sales, but only on our website. If you have a mobile phone, you could download our app and reserve your seats now.

M : I forgot about that. I actually have the app on my phone. I'll check it out right now.

41. (　　) Where is the conversation taking place?
  (A) At a library.
  (B) At a museum.
  (C) At a theater.
  (D) At a supermarket.

42. (　　) Why does the woman apologize?
  (A) A website is not accessible.
  (B) An event has been canceled.
  (C) Some tickets are unavailable.
  (D) Some prices have increased.

GO ON TO THE NEXT PAGE.

43. (　　) What does the man say he will do next?
- (A) Call a manager.
- (B) Register a complaint.
- (C) Go to a different location.
- (D) Visit a website.

Questions 44 through 46 *refer to the following conversation with three speakers.*

Man US : Excuse me, ma'am. Did we hear your announcement over the airport loudspeakers correctly? You're looking for passengers to volunteer to take a later flight to Sacramento?

W : Unfortunately, the 3:30 flight is overbooked. So, if you don't mind departing at 7:45 tonight, I can give you a voucher for $200 off a future flight.

Man US : Well, since the tech convention doesn't start until tomorrow, perhaps my colleague and I wouldn't mind getting the discount coupon. Roger, do you agree?

Man UK : Absolutely. In fact, Dave, we skipped lunch, didn't we? So it will be a great chance to grab dinner.

W : I recommend the Thai restaurant in Terminal 1. The food and atmosphere are top notch.

44. (　　) Where is the conversation taking place?
- (A) At a travel agency.
- (B) In a hotel.
- (C) In an airport.
- (D) At a restaurant.

45. (　　) According to the woman, what will the men receive?
- (A) A seating upgrade.
- (B) A discount voucher.
- (C) A parking permit.
- (D) A travel guidebook.

46. (　　) What will the men most likely do next?
- (A) Give a presentation.
- (B) Eat at a restaurant.
- (C) Return to their workplace.
- (D) Change the hotel reservation.

Questions 47 through 49 *refer to the following conversation.*

M : Hey, Diane. Glad I caught up with you. Listen... You're aware of the management meeting tomorrow about the budget for next quarter? So... the accounting department's expense proposal?

W : I know, Ted. It's just been rather hectic in accounting lately, and the report... The main sticking point is the estimated cost of computer equipment and upgrades for our new hires. Based on the number of new employees, we're going to be spending way more than usual. But it's hard to say exactly how much.

M : I get that. We have some flexibility for increasing our spending right now. We're all aware of the increase in staff, so... Let's see what the other managers can do about renegotiating our contract with Tacer Electronics. Hopefully, we can get a better deal.

47. (   ) What does the man mean by, "So...the accounting expense proposal"?
    (A) He wants to know if a document is ready.
    (B) He wants to extend a deadline.
    (C) He wants to know if schedule has been changed.
    (D) He wants an explanation for a policy decision.

48. (   ) What does the woman say about an expense estimate?
    (A) It has been misplaced.
    (B) It will be higher than expected.
    (C) It was already approved.
    (D) It contained some mistakes.

49. (   ) What will the man discuss at a meeting?
    (A) Contracts with vendors.
    (B) Design modifications.
    (C) Accounting practices.
    (D) Candidates for a career promotion.

***Questions 50 through 52** refer to the following conversation.*

W : Gabe, all the news reports are saying the big snowstorm heading our way may disrupt bus and train service tomorrow, and I'm scheduled to open the store.

M : I know, Paola. Sounds like it's going to be a major storm, and most of our employees use public transportation. So, I'm thinking about closing the store tomorrow altogether, but want to keep an eye on the weather reports. I'll make a decision before closing tonight.

W : Let me know if you need help contacting the rest of the staff.

M : Will do. Thanks for your care and concern, Paola.

50. (   ) What problem does the woman mention?
    (A) Parking in the area is limited.
    (B) The sales forecast is negative.
    (C) Customer complaints have increased.
    (D) Bad weather has been predicted.

GO ON TO THE NEXT PAGE.

51. (　　) What does the man say he will decide this evening?
　　　　(A) When to launch a new sales promotion.
　　　　(B) When to meet with investors.
　　　　(C) Whether the store will be closed.
　　　　(D) Whether additional employees should be hired.

52. (　　) What does the woman offer to help the man with?
　　　　(A) Organizing a carpool.
　　　　(B) Revising a work schedule.
　　　　(C) Contacting employees.
　　　　(D) Opening the store.

Questions 53 through 55 *refer to the following conversation.*

W : Excuse me. I saw some headphones on display and I want to know how much they cost. Can you help me?
M : Sure! Which pair of headphones is it?

W : These red Sonic Blasters. They sound great. But this pair doesn't have a price tag.
M : Oh yeah. <u>Those are nice.</u> The price tag should be on the box.

W : Actually, the box isn't on the shelf.
M : That's strange. Anyway, I'll look up the price in our system. Give me a minute.

53. (　　) What does the woman ask the man about?
　　　　(A) The price of an item.
　　　　(B) The location of a store.
　　　　(C) The maker of a product.
　　　　(D) The availability of colors.

54. (　　) Why does the man say, "Those are nice"?
　　　　(A) To convince a friend to buy headphones.
　　　　(B) To suggest an alternative product.
　　　　(C) To compliment a co-worker.
　　　　(D) To express agreement.

55. (　　) What does the man say he will do?
　　　　(A) Find a comparable item.
　　　　(B) Check a price list.
　　　　(C) Print a receipt.
　　　　(D) Provide a coupon code.

M : Yeah, hi. This is Bruce Wright. I ordered a vacuum cleaner from you guys three days ago. I paid for next day shipping and it hasn't arrived yet. The tracking number is HOV283. Would you mind letting me know what's happened to it?

W : Mr. Wright, thanks for calling. Okay, let me run that tracking number. Yes, my system indicates that a delivery was attempted yesterday at 301 North Elm Street in Berkeley. The driver reported no one home to accept delivery.

M : But, that's my home address! I specifically indicated an alternate delivery address. Why didn't the driver call me? My phone number is on the invoice.

W : You're right. It appears the vacuum cleaner was automatically sent to your billing address. I apologize for that. Let me confirm your information now so that I can reschedule the delivery. To compensate for the inconvenience, I'll have it sent priority, and refund the delivery fee to your credit card.

56. (   ) Why is the man calling?
    (A) To schedule a repair.
    (B) To inquire about a bill.
    (C) To check the status of an order.
    (D) To provide an updated credit card number.

57. (   ) What problem does the woman mention?
    (A) A product was sent to the wrong address.
    (B) A product is no longer available.
    (C) A deadline was missed.
    (D) A credit card payment was not received.

58. (   ) What does the woman offer to do?
    (A) Speak with a supervisor.
    (B) Issue a refund.
    (C) Change a password.
    (D) Add a warranty.

Questions 59 through 61 _refer to the following conversation with three speakers._

Woman US : Oh good, you're both here. We need to plan our strategy for next month's travel fair in Chicago. So, what should we focus on first?

Woman UK : Well, our travel agency only has a booth at the fair for two days. That's not a lot of time to make a big impression.

M : I think we should develop a brochure that highlights some of our most popular tours and destinations. Can you put that together with me, Sophia?

GO ON TO THE NEXT PAGE.

Woman UK : Yes, but we're under a tight deadline. It has to be sent to the printers by next week in order to have it in time for the travel fair.

59. (   ) What is the conversation mainly about?
    (A) Finding a guest speaker for a convention.
    (B) Creating an employee handbook.
    (C) Organizing a training session.
    (D) Preparing for a business exposition.

60. (   ) What does the man suggest doing?
    (A) Reserving more time.
    (B) Revising a timetable.
    (C) Sending out invitations.
    (D) Making a brochure.

61. (   ) What does Sophia say she is concerned about?
    (A) A canceled reservation.
    (B) An unconfirmed meeting.
    (C) An approaching deadline.
    (D) An incorrect report.

Questions 62 through 64 *refer to the following conversation and floor plan.*

M : Good morning, welcome to Ruby's Books and Café. Can I help you find something in particular?

W : Yes, I need a copy of a book called *The Rise of Social Media*. My friends and I are starting a book club next month. I've heard it's a fascinating read and a good title for discussion.

M : No doubt. Social media is a hot topic these days. Anyway, you can find it on the first floor on the back wall of the store next to the café. Almost all our books are arranged by author. Can I interest you in a cup of coffee in our café?

W : No, thanks, but I think I'll browse for a little while.

62. (   ) Who most likely is the man?
    (A) A sales clerk.
    (B) A baker.
    (C) An author.
    (D) A teacher.

63. (   ) What does the woman say she heard about the book?
    (A) It will provide opportunities for discussion.
    (B) It is the first book in a series.
    (C) It has been a best-seller for many months.
    (D) It was written by an associate.

64. (   ) Look at the graphic. In which section is the book that the woman is looking for?
  (A) Travel.
  (B) Reference.
  (C) Non-fiction.
  (D) Young Adult.

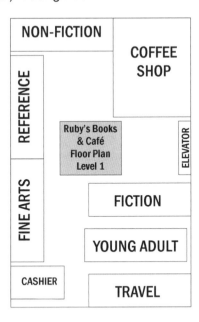

Questions 65 through 67 _refer to the following conversation and review._

W : The new issue of _Franklin County Living Magazine_ is out. I guess you've seen the article
   with the list of the best local restaurants? The article gave our restaurant five stars in the
   category of customer service. As the general manager, you must be proud.
M : Well, I think the article confirms it was a good decision to hire more staff this spring. It
   shows that customers appreciate attentive service.

W : True, but I'm disappointed that some of our ratings weren't better. I'm not surprised that we
   scored low in the menu options category, but I am surprised by this one, where we received
   only two stars. We'll have to address that area of concern as soon as possible.
M : Yes, it may be a good idea to meet with the owners. We have no control over that. <u>They
   may be willing to make a few compromises.</u>

65. (   ) Who is the man?
  (A) An editor.
  (B) A manager.
  (C) A financial consultant.
  (D) A food critic.

GO ON TO THE NEXT PAGE.

66. (   ) Look at the graphic. What area does the woman want the restaurant to improve in?
   (A) Customer service.
   (B) Menu options.
   (C) Atmosphere.
   (D) Prices and value.

Silk Road Restaurant Rating

Atmosphere
✪ ✪ ✪ ✪
Prices and value
✪ ✪
Customer service
✪ ✪ ✪ ✪ ✪
Menu options
✪ ✪ ✪

67. (   ) What does the man mean when he says, "They may be willing to make a few compromises"?
   (A) The owners may agree to lower prices.
   (B) The owners may wish to expand the business.
   (C) The critics may welcome another visit.
   (D) The staff may appreciate the time off.

Questions 68 through 70 _refer to the following conversation and picture._

W : In this afternoon's lab training session, we'll discuss monitoring the barometer batteries. If the power's too low, we won't know the exact pressure within the lab. This is incredibly important when conducting research.

M : Do the barometers use an independent power source or run on batteries?

W : Batteries. And that's the most important point. You'll need to monitor the battery closely; always check the display screen.

M : When do the batteries need to be replaced?

W : As described in your trainee manual, the battery power levels will be displayed on the unit. Replace batteries when they reach 25 percent. We don't want to swap them out any earlier than we have to, but we'll lose valuable time and data if the barometers need to be reset.

68. (   ) What event is taking place?

    (A) A sales meeting.

    (B) An award ceremony.

    (C) A training session.

    (D) A weather forecast.

69. (   ) What does the man ask about?

    (A) Additional safety procedures.

    (B) Different lab facilities.

    (C) Experiment results.

    (D) Alternative power sources.

70. (   ) Look at the graphic. According to the woman, how many bars will be displayed when the battery should be replaced?

    (A) Three bars.

    (B) Two bars.

    (C) One bar.

    (D) Zero bars.

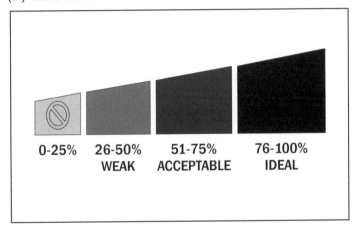

GO ON TO THE NEXT PAGE.

PART 4

Questions 71 through 73 *refer to the following excerpt from a meeting.*

The last item on the agenda for this managers' meeting concerns the transition to our new dispatch tracking software. The new version of the program is significantly more sophisticated than the one we've been using. This software will allow us to track every single driver in our fleet, regardless of where they are or where they're heading. This will benefit our customers by reducing the time it takes to book a taxi. We will start training dispatchers on using the software next week. Ms. Leslie Eastman, a trainer from the software company, will be on site all week to do the training.

71. (　) According to the speaker, what will be changing at the company?
   (A) How drivers' hours are scheduled.
   (B) How drivers are tracked.
   (C) How customer complaints are handled.
   (D) How reservations are submitted.

72. (　) What will the company be able to do for customers?
   (A) Reduce wait times.
   (B) Extend service routes.
   (C) Lower prices.
   (D) Offer more products.

73. (　) What will Ms. Eastman be doing?
   (A) Conducting a survey.
   (B) Inspecting vehicles.
   (C) Testing equipment.
   (D) Training employees.

Questions 74 through 76 *refer to the following telephone message.*

Hi, my name is Jeff Sweeney and I'm calling about an issue... I ride the Sheffield Line from Halston Street station every morning around 7:00, headed downtown. This morning, I, along with dozens of other people, waited over an hour on the platform before giving up and taking a taxi. There was no announcement or explanation for the delay, and no agent working the station. Then, I checked your company's website for news about delays, but there wasn't any current information posted. So... I decided to call this information hotline. Can you tell me if there's been a change to the Sheffield Line train schedule? I need to know today, please, before my workday ends. My phone number is 727-0987. Thanks.

74. (   ) What business is the speaker calling?
   (A) A dentist's office.
   (B) A shoe repair shop.
   (C) A transportation service.
   (D) A travel agency.

75. (   ) Why did the speaker take a taxi?
   (A) He was concerned about parking.
   (B) He was late for a dinner date.
   (C) His car broke down.
   (D) His train never arrived.

76. (   ) What would the speaker like to know?
   (A) How to get to an event.
   (B) Whether a schedule has changed.
   (C) When a new service will begin.
   (D) How much a membership will cost.

Questions 77 through 79 refer to the following telephone message.

Hi, this is Jennifer from Storch Real Estate. There's a new warehouse space that just came on the market that we haven't listed yet. I think you'd really like it. It's in the heart of the industrial district, just like you wanted. The only problem may be that the rent is higher than your initial range, but the warehouse space is much larger than the others we've seen. You mentioned expanding your business, and so I knew it would be something you'd be interested in. Now, I'll need you to let me know as soon as you get this message if you want to see it. I won't list the property until I hear back from you, but I can't hold it for too long.

77. (   ) Who most likely is the speaker?
   (A) A real estate agent.
   (B) A legal advisor.
   (C) An architect.
   (D) A banker.

GO ON TO THE NEXT PAGE

78. (   ) What does the speaker say is a problem?
    (A) Some construction has not been completed.
    (B) A warehouse is difficult to find.
    (C) An inspection will be postponed.
    (D) A price is higher than desired.

79. (   ) What does the speaker ask the listener to do?
    (A) Submit a deposit.
    (B) Sign a waiver.
    (C) Return the call promptly.
    (D) Review a document carefully.

Questions 80 through 82 *refer to the following broadcast.*

Good afternoon, here's your WGBH-FM 105.9 traffic report. For anyone heading downtown, there are 20 to 30-minute delays entering the central business district, and traffic is backed up on the circle interchange. As you know, our city is hosting the annual bluegrass music festival this weekend. It will kick off this evening at Citgo Mobile Arena, and although there are some tickets left, it's expected to sell out. So, if you have to commute into the city this weekend, we strongly encourage you to take the bus or the train.

80. (   ) What is the main topic of the broadcast?
    (A) A celebrity interview.
    (B) A weather report.
    (C) A traffic update.
    (D) An international news story.

81. (   ) According to the speaker, what will begin today?
    (A) A sports tournament.
    (B) A music festival.
    (C) A conference.
    (D) A seasonal market.

82. (   ) What does the speaker suggest that listeners do?
    (A) Arrive early.
    (B) Bring warm clothes.
    (C) Purchase tickets online.
    (D) Take public transportation.

Questions 83 through 85 refer to the following announcement.

Let's wrap up our weekly personnel department meeting with a staffing update for the St. Louis office. As you know, we've been working hard to fill several managerial positions there by the end of the year. And our policy is, of course, to promote from within. However, so far, most of the applications from qualified candidates are from outside the company, and, well, the deadline to submit was May 15. So, in light of the situation, I want the team to start interviewing those few in-house candidates next week. Please refer to the interview schedule, which I emailed to all of you at the outset of this meeting.

83. (   ) Who most likely is the speaker?
    (A) A computer programmer.
    (B) A personnel manager.
    (C) An accountant.
    (D) A real estate agent.

84. (   ) What does the speaker mean when she says, "The deadline to submit was May 15"?
    (A) They missed a good hiring opportunity.
    (B) They need to verify some details.
    (C) They must move forward with a task.
    (D) They forgot to notify a colleague.

85. (   ) According to the speaker, what will happen next week?
    (A) A policy will be implemented.
    (B) Interviews will begin.
    (C) Bonuses will increase.
    (D) A system upgrade will be completed.

Questions 86 through 88 refer to the following advertisement.

Do you regularly use teleconferencing to connect with colleagues working in other locations? Introducing Corona Flash, an easy teleconferencing service at a fraction of the cost! Our service is a simple way to set up and conduct conference calls in the U.S., Canada, and around the world. Teleconferencing should be easy and a conferencing company should be honest. That's why we've never had any hidden fees, contracts, or monthly charges. Collaborate with groups from anywhere, to anywhere, anytime. Corona Flash — We're the next level of audio conference calling service. Visit our website to watch a step-by-step video of how easy it is to use.

GO ON TO THE NEXT PAGE.

86. (   ) What is Corona Flash?
      (A) A store security system.
      (B) An Internet service provider.
      (C) A teleconferencing application.
      (D) A new brand of smartphone.

87. (   ) What does the speaker mean when he says, "Teleconferencing should be easy and a conferencing company should be honest"?
      (A) Employees need more training.
      (B) Networks should be faster.
      (C) An invoice should be reviewed.
      (D) Other systems are not as efficient.

88. (   ) What does the speaker say listeners can do on a website?
      (A) Register a product.
      (B) Make a purchase.
      (C) View a demonstration.
      (D) Sign up for updates.

Questions 89 through 91 refer to the following excerpt from a meeting.

I wanted to end our monthly staff meeting on a high note. Now, if you haven't read the business section in today's *Cleveland Daily News*, I highly recommend that you do. You'll see there that we received the award for the best digital marketing company in the Greater Cleveland area. But keep in mind, there are new firms opening every day. In order to remain successful, our business has to grow. And so, we've leased a larger space and will be hiring more people soon. Details of our move and expansion should be finalized by the end of the month.

89. (   ) What did the *Cleveland Daily News* recently do?
      (A) It announced award winners.
      (B) It merged with another newspaper.
      (C) It reviewed a group of restaurants.
      (D) It reduced its subscription fee.

90. (   ) What has the business done recently?
      (A) Bought a new property.
      (B) Leased a larger facility.
      (C) Hired more staff.
      (D) Upgraded some computers.

91. (　　) What does the speaker imply when he says, "There are new firms opening every day"?
　　(A) A branch location will be built.
　　(B) Competition for customers will increase.
　　(C) More people will move to the area.
　　(D) Road conditions will worsen.

Questions 92 through 94 *refer to the following announcement.*

Greetings and welcome Spring Hill Mall shoppers! I'd like to direct your attention to the main atrium of our shopping mall today. In just 10 minutes, we're inviting you to join us there for a professional cooking demonstration. We'll be showcasing a variety of home cookware from different stores here in the mall. After the show, there'll be culinary experts on hand for those who have questions about cooking and how to buy and maintain the proper cookware. And, one of the housewares companies participating, Uptown Pantry, has just set up a new store on the ground floor. You're invited to attend their grand opening today.

92. (　　) Where is the announcement taking place?
　　(A) At a catering company headquarters.
　　(B) At a sports stadium.
　　(C) At a shopping mall.
　　(D) At a restaurant.

93. (　　) What does the speaker say will happen immediately after today's event?
　　(A) Experts will provide consultations.
　　(B) Attendees will fill out a survey.
　　(C) A famous chef will speak.
　　(D) A meal will be served.

94. (　　) What does the speaker say about Uptown Pantry?
　　(A) It has won an award.
　　(B) It has undergone a renovation.
　　(C) It is now officially open.
　　(D) It is giving away free tickets.

GO ON TO THE NEXT PAGE.

Guys, just a quick roundup before we open the bakery today. If you take a look at this chart, you'll see this week's winning pastry. As promised, the bakery item that got the most votes will be discounted by 25% for a week. I'd like to thank Daniel again for his creative idea of holding this weekly contest. Our customers are crazy about this promotion, and it has really increased sales. I know a lot of you have great ideas, too. Remember, you guys are always welcome to share.

95. (   ) Look at the graphic. Which item will be discounted this week?
   (A) Cupcake.
   (B) Doughnut.
   (C) Scone.
   (D) Muffin.

BAKERY ITEM	# of votes
Muffin	503
Éclair	411
Scone	392
Doughnut	225
Cupcake	144

96. (   ) Why does the speaker thank Daniel?
   (A) He proposed a sales promotion.
   (B) He developed new bakery items.
   (C) He worked extra hours.
   (D) He submitted an order.

97. (   ) What does the speaker remind the listeners to do?
   (A) Make some suggestions.
   (B) Sign up for a task.
   (C) Clean some equipment.
   (D) Count customer votes.

Hello, this is the automated call service from Syracuse Water and Gas reminding you that your utility bill was due Monday, April 12. Since your payment is ten days overdue, a late fee has been added to your account balance. Please pay the bill plus your ten-day late fee on our website at: "http://www.syracuse.gov". We also offer an auto payment feature on our website. If you sign up for this service, you will be required to provide a credit card or bank account number. After that, your future bills will be paid automatically on the day they are due. If you have questions about this option, please call us at 717-922-7080. Thank you.

98. (   ) Where does the speaker most likely work?
   (A) At a financial institution.
   (B) At a water park.
   (C) At a utility company.
   (D) At a bank.

99. (   ) Look at the graphic. How much is the listener's late fee?
   (A) $5.99.
   (B) $12.98.
   (C) $21.97.
   (D) $30.96.

Late Payment Policy	
Days Overdue	Fee
5	$5.99
10	$12.98
15	$21.97
20	$30.96

100. (   ) What must the listener provide to sign up for a service?
   (A) A medical certificate.
   (B) An identification card.
   (C) Some contact information.
   (D) Some payment details.

GO ON TO THE NEXT PAGE

NO TEST MATERIAL ON THIS PAGE

New TOEIC Speaking Test

Question 1: Read a Text Aloud

 **Question 1**

Directions: In this part of the test, you will read aloud the text on the screen. You will have 45 seconds to prepare. Then you will have 45 seconds to read the text aloud.

Unlike company-employed agents, independent insurance agents and insurance brokers represent more than one insurance company, so they can offer clients a wider choice of auto, home, business, life, and health coverage as well as retirement and employee-benefit products. Independent agents and brokers not only advise clients about insurance. They also recommend loss-prevention ideas that can cut costs. If a loss occurs, the independent insurance agent or broker stands with the client until the claim is settled.

PREPARATION TIME
00 : 00 : 45

RESPONSE TIME
00 : 00 : 45

GO ON TO THE NEXT PAGE

Question 2: Read a Text Aloud

((**5**)) **Question 2**

Directions: In this part of the test, you will read aloud the text on the screen. You will have 45 seconds to prepare. Then you will have 45 seconds to read the text aloud.

A few years ago, our company had to decide whether or not we wanted to move to the suburbs, where it would be less expensive and easier to expand, or stay in our long-time home, urban Seattle. The answer was quite obvious—we decided to stay in the city for a multitude of reasons. One of my favorite reasons why we chose to stay in Seattle is because we want to be connected to this vibrant, growing community. Staying in the city also affords us the opportunity to strengthen our partnerships with some of our nonprofit neighbors.

PREPARATION TIME
00 : 00 : 45

RESPONSE TIME
00 : 00 : 45

Question 3: Describe a Picture

 **Question 3**

Directions: In this part of the test, you will describe the picture on your screen in as much detail as you can. You will have 30 seconds to prepare your response. Then you will have 45 seconds to speak about the picture.

PREPARATION TIME
00 : 00 : 30

RESPONSE TIME
00 : 00 : 45

GO ON TO THE NEXT PAGE.

Question 3: Describe a Picture

答題範例

 **Question 3**

The people are in a cleaning shop.

The business is most likely a dry cleaners.

The shop offers professional cleaning of clothing.

There are three people in the frame.

One woman is a customer.

She appears to be paying for some services.

Another woman is at the cash register.

She has very large earrings.

She's also wearing a baseball cap.

The third woman is over by the far counter.

She's obscured by a large metal hanging rack.

She's most likely preparing clothes that have been cleaned.

There are several racks in the background.

Most of them contain clean clothing.

The clothes are wrapped in plastic.

There are clothes on the counter in front of the customer.

A sign in the background advertises a particular service.

The customer has her back to the camera.

Questions 4-6: Respond to Questions

 **Question 4**

Directions: In this part of the test, you will answer three questions. For each question, begin responding immediately after you hear a beep. No preparation time is provided. You will have 15 seconds to respond to Questions 4 and 5 and 30 seconds to respond to Question 6.

Imagine that you are talking to a friend on the telephone.

Question 4

What did you do last weekend and with whom did you do it?

RESPONSE TIME
00 : 00 : 15

Question 5

What do you have planned this weekend?

RESPONSE TIME
00 : 00 : 15

Question 6

My cousins are coming to visit this weekend, but I haven't made any plans. What do you suggest I do with them?

RESPONSE TIME
00 : 00 : 30

GO ON TO THE NEXT PAGE.

Questions 4-6: Respond to Questions

答題範例

 **Question 4**

What did you do last weekend and with whom did you do it?

Answer

> I went camping with some friends.
>
> The campsite is up north in the woods.
>
> We spent two nights in a log cabin.

 **Question 5**

What do you have planned this weekend?

Answer

> Nothing special.
>
> I'm going to take it easy.
>
> I'm tired from last weekend.

Questions 4-6: Respond to Questions

((6)) **Question 6**

My cousins are coming to visit this weekend, but I haven't made any plans.
What do you suggest I do with them?

Answer

Well, you could start with a visit to a night market.

The night market is fun and interesting.

Your cousins might enjoy that.

There's also a music festival on Elephant Mountain.

It starts on Friday afternoon and runs through Sunday.

If they like music, that would be cool.

You should consider going on a hike.

There are many great hiking trails around the city.

That way, your cousins can appreciate some of the local

natural beauty.

GO ON TO THE NEXT PAGE

Questions 7-9: Respond to Questions Using Information Provided

 **Question 7**

Directions: In this part of the test, you will answer three questions based on the information provided. You will have 30 seconds to read the information before the questions begin. For each question, begin responding immediately after you hear a beep. No additional preparation time is provided. You will have 15 seconds to respond to Questions 7 and 8 and 30 seconds to respond to Question 9.

Columbia Farmers Market

When: March 17 (8:00 am – 12:00 pm)
Where: Parkade Center, Northeast Parking Lot C
Contact: Corrina Smith
Phone: 573-823-6889
Website: http://www.columbiafarmersmarket.org

Experience the taste of mid-Missouri at the Columbia Farmers Market! Find us every Saturday from 8 am to noon (mid-March–mid-November) in our new temporary location, the northeast Parkade Center's parking lot (601 Business Loop 70W).

Fresh vegetables & fruit, meat, farm fresh eggs, cheeses, honey, cut flowers, plants, artisan items & more. As a producer-only market, everything sold here is offered by the farmers and artisans who help sustain our region. SNAP (food stamps) accepted at all markets. Live music every Saturday! Rain or Shine!

Groundbreaking should take place this spring at the Clary-Shy Agriculture Park. While construction takes place, we will be setting up in the northeast lot at Parkade Center. Make sure to follow our social media pages to stay up-to-date on the progress.

Hi, I'm interested in the Farmers Market. Would you mind if I asked a few questions?

PREPARATION TIME
00 : 00 : 30

Question 7	Question 8	Question 9
RESPONSE TIME	RESPONSE TIME	RESPONSE TIME
00 : 00 : 15	00 : 00 : 15	00 : 00 : 30

Questions 7-9: Respond to Questions Using Information Provided

答題範例

 **Question 7**

When and where does the event take place?

Answer

> The Farmers Market takes place every Saturday.
>
> It starts at 8:00 AM and ends around noon.
>
> It's held in the Northeast Parking Lot C of Parkade Center.

 **Question 8**

Is the market always held in this location?

Answer

> No.
>
> The northeast Parkade Center's parking lot is a temporary
>
> location.
>
> Our permanent spot at the Clary-Shy Agriculture Park will
>
> open this spring.

GO ON TO THE NEXT PAGE

Questions 7-9: Respond to Questions Using Information Provided

((◖ 6 ◗)) **Question 9**

What can I expect to find at the market, or, is there anything else I should know?

Answer

Well, first of all, everything sold at the market is from a

local producer or artisan.

So, these are the same people that help sustain our

region.

The market is a celebration of their bounty.

You'll find farm-fresh fruit and vegetables.

You'll find honey and cheese.

You'll also find hand-crafted artisan products.

Finally, you'll find flowers and plants.

We also have a live band.

We accept food stamps, too.

Question 10: Propose a Solution

 **Question 10**

Directions: In this part of the test, you will be presented with a problem and asked to propose a solution. You will have 30 seconds to prepare. Then you will have 60 seconds to speak. In your response, be sure to show that you recognize the problem, and propose a way of dealing with the problem.

In your response, be sure to

• show that you recognize the caller's problem, and

• propose a way of dealing with the problem.

PREPARATION TIME
00 : 00 : 30

RESPONSE TIME
00 : 01 : 00

GO ON TO THE NEXT PAGE

Question 10: Propose a Solution

答題範例

 **Question 10**

Voice Message

> Hello, Derek? It's Grace Peterson calling from Human Resources. I know we're scheduled to meet tomorrow afternoon to go over the revised insurance plans for part-time employees, but I won't be able to make it. Some new hires are starting tomorrow, and I was asked to show them around the building. The revisions are now complete and all plans fall within the guidelines. Since I know you're waiting on this information, do you mind asking Richard to fill you in? He's just as familiar with the plan as I am, if not more so.

Question 10: Propose a Solution

答題範例

Hi Grace, I got your message.

I understand that you cannot attend the meeting tomorrow.

I heard that we have some new hires coming on board.

The revisions are indeed important.

I'll need them to balance the budget.

The sooner I get them, the better.

I'll try to get a hold of Richard.

He's been busy lately and hasn't returned my calls.

Would you remind him to contact me?

Meanwhile, I have another idea.

Why don't you e-mail me the revisions?

That way, we can eliminate one step of the process.

I don't think it will be necessary for Richard to fill me in.

I'm familiar with the plans.

So, I think that would be the best course of action.

I'll look for your e-mail.

Thanks for your help.

Have a great tomorrow.

GO ON TO THE NEXT PAGE

Question 11: Express an Opinion

 **Question 11**

Directions: In this part of the test, you will give your opinion about a specific topic. Be sure to say as much as you can in the time allowed. You will have 15 seconds to prepare. Then you will have 60 seconds to speak.

In general, people are living longer now. Discuss the causes of this phenomenon. Use specific reasons and details to develop your answer.

PREPARATION TIME
00 : 00 : 15

RESPONSE TIME
00 : 01 : 00

Question 11: Express an Opinion

答題範例

 **Question 11**

The three big reasons that people are living longer lives are: food supply and nutrition, health, and hygiene.

All three have seen major improvements in standards since the nineteenth and early twentieth centuries.

However, another important factor is knowing their importance to our health and life expectancy.

By taking necessary steps we can ensure a healthy lifestyle.

Our access to information has also improved as a result of scientific research.

Methods of information dissemination, for example, the Internet, have increased dramatically.

For example, the packaging of food products must display the nutritional content of food.

Some products use color-coding so that we know whether they are good for us.

The importance of eating a balanced diet is widely known.

Government websites provide information about the lifestyle choices we can make in order to reduce our risk of developing diseases.

The dangers of smoking cigarettes are included on packaging.

Smoking is banned in most public places, and the age limit has been raised to 18 years.

Advertisements on buses and tubes inform us of the importance of washing our hands.

There are signs reminding us to cover our mouths when we cough or sneeze.

Health and safety legislation provides strict regulations for hygiene in restaurants, hospitals and factories

But following a healthy lifestyle is still a choice that we make, and not everyone chooses it or is able to do so.

The real phenomenon of longevity is people with terrible lifestyles who live to be 100 years old.

Therefore, there must be some kind of a genetic component involved.

Not to be overlooked, vaccinations have probably done more for life expectancy than any one factor.

People are no longer getting wiped out by epidemics like polio.

In my opinion, improvements in medical care are the main reason people live so long.

GO ON TO THE NEXT PAGE

NO TEST MATERIAL ON THIS PAGE

New TOEIC Writing Test

Questions 1-5: Write a Sentence Based on a Picture

Question 1

Directions: Write ONE sentence based on the picture using the TWO words or phrases under it. You may change the forms of the words and you may use them in any order.

woman / drive

答題範例：**A woman is driving a bus.**

GO ON TO THE NEXT PAGE

Questions 1-5: Write a Sentence Based on a Picture

Question 2

Directions: Write ONE sentence based on the picture using the TWO words or phrases under it. You may change the forms of the words and you may use them in any order.

hikers / descend

答題範例：**The hikers are descending a hill.**

Questions 1-5: Write a Sentence Based on a Picture

Question 3

Directions: Write ONE sentence based on the picture using the TWO words or phrases under it. You may change the forms of the words and you may use them in any order.

seat / meeting

答題範例：**Some men are seated for a meeting.**

GO ON TO THE NEXT PAGE

Questions 1-5: Write a Sentence Based on a Picture

Question 4

Directions: Write ONE sentence based on the picture using the TWO words or phrases under it. You may change the forms of the words and you may use them in any order.

road / truck

答題範例：**There are several trucks on the side of the road.**

Questions 1-5: Write a Sentence Based on a Picture

Question 5

Directions: Write ONE sentence based on the picture using the TWO words or phrases under it. You may change the forms of the words and you may use them in any order.

men / sign

答題範例：**Three men are standing next to a sign.**

GO ON TO THE NEXT PAGE.

Questions 6-7: Respond to a written request

Question 6

Directions: Read the e-mail below.

From: Rondell Clayburn
To: Rebecca Christiansen
Re: Program change
Sent: July 16

Dear Ms. Christiansen,

I am looking forward to meeting you at the 8th Annual International Conference on International Trade in just two short days!

You had inquired about the possibility of moving your talk to an earlier time slot. We have just had a cancellation. Moira Brown has a scheduling conflict and has requested to give her talk later in the day. Therefore, her 10:30 slot on Day 1 is available. With your approval, I would like to move your talk to that time.

I need to know whether you will be using the computer provided by the conference center or whether you will need to connect your own computer to the projector. Also, will you require Internet access during your talk? Please let me know at your earliest convenience.

Sincerely yours,

Rondell Clayburn
Chairman, Organizing Committee
8th Annual International Conference on International Trade

Directions: Write back to Mr. Clayburn as Ms. Christiansen. AGREE to the time change and answer BOTH of his questions.

Questions 6-7: Respond to a written request

答題範例

Question 6

Mr. Clayburn,

Thank you for your message, and I'm looking forward to meeting you at the conference as well. In regards to the proposed program change, 10:30 on Day 1 would work perfectly for me. I approve the change and will plan to appear accordingly.

I will be bringing my own computer, and yes, Internet access would be greatly appreciated. I will also bring my own Wi-Fi hotspot, just in case.

Again, thank you and I'll see you on Friday.

Sincerely,
Rebecca Christiansen

GO ON TO THE NEXT PAGE

Questions 6-7: Respond to a written request

Question 7

Directions: Read the e-mail below.

From: Mark Clark
To: Sally Kimmock
Date: Thursday, July 23
Subject: Job Reference

Dear Ms. Kimmock,

As one of your former students at Crestford Academy of Culinary Arts, I need to ask a favor of you. I am applying for a position at The Oceanaire Seafood Room in Baltimore and would like to know if I may use you as a reference since your class was most relevant to the job. Please let me know at your earliest convenience. I would like to submit my application by the end of this week and need to include my references in the online application. I have attached a document for you to review. It includes both the job description and my resume.

Thank you again for your instruction. I enjoyed being in your class.

Mark Clark

Directions: Reply as Sally Kimmock and **AGREE** to Mark Clark's request. Give **ONE** reason why he would be a good candidate for the job, and **ONE** suggestion about his application and resume.

Questions 6-7: Respond to a written request

答題範例

Question 7

Mark,

I would be happy to serve as a reference. You picked up the information presented in our class very quickly, so I think you'll be a good fit for a fast-paced environment like The Oceanaire Seafood Room. I reviewed your resume and just wanted to remind you that the class was one that contributes to a certificate. You completed the program in June, so you should indicate that you earned a Level II ACF certification.

Best wishes!

Sally Kimmock

GO ON TO THE NEXT PAGE

Questions 8: Write an opinion essay

Question 8

Directions: Read the question below. You have 30 minutes to plan, write, and revise your essay. Typically, an effective response will contain a minimum of 300 words.

Neighbors are the people who live near us. In your opinion, what are the qualities of a good neighbor? Use specific details and examples in your answer.

Questions 8: Write an opinion essay

答題範例

Question 8

Taipei is a densely populated city with many people literally living on top of each other. Therefore, almost everybody lives in an apartment with neighbors in close proximity, in every direction—up, down, across, and behind. In this situation, it is important to know how to be a good neighbor.

First of all, good neighbors are quiet. Anyone who has ever lived next to noisy neighbors can attest to this. Good neighbors are aware that there are other people living in the building and keep noise to a minimum. They don't scream or blare music or throw parties until late hours in the evening. They don't slam doors and yell in the hallways. They show some respect for those around them.

Next, good neighbors respect their community. Anyone who leaves garbage or junk in the hallways, in the parking lot or in other common areas is not a good neighbor. A neighbor who allows his or her junk to accumulate in shared spaces shows disrespect for everyone else in the building. Good neighbors show common courtesy and regularly take out their trash and keep shared and public areas clean.

Additionally, good neighbors handle situations maturely. If a good neighbor has a problem with someone, for example, a tenant whose dog has been barking a lot recently, he or she would kindly approach the person about the matter. Likewise, he or she takes into account the concerns of others who may object to his or her own behavior. Everyone gets along better and problems are solved faster when people behave like mature adults. Bad neighbors don't handle situations maturely. They ignore others, respond rudely or turn to passive aggressive retaliation methods. Good neighbors never behave that way.

What's more, good neighbors help when and where they can. There isn't a rule stating that good neighbors should lend a helping hand, but in general, they do. Good neighbors let you borrow a key to the downstairs laundry room when you've misplaced yours. Good neighbors will team up with you to speak with the landlord about a maintenance issue in the common stairwell. Ultimately, they're looking to reside in a pleasant, friendly and safe environment, too.

No matter what one's living situation is, having good neighbors is important. The best way to find good neighbors is to first be a good neighbor to others.

TOEIC 練習測驗 答案紙

LISTENING SECTION

Part 1

No.	ANSWER
1	A B C D
2	A B C D
3	A B C D
4	A B C D
5	A B C D
6	A B C D
7	A B C D
8	A B C D
9	A B C D
10	A B C D

Part 2

No.	ANSWER	No.	ANSWER
11	A B C	21	A B C
12	A B C	22	A B C
13	A B C	23	A B C
14	A B C	24	A B C
15	A B C	25	A B C
16	A B C	26	A B C
17	A B C	27	A B C
18	A B C	28	A B C
19	A B C	29	A B C
20	A B C	30	A B C

Part 3

No.	ANSWER	No.	ANSWER
31	A B C D	41	A B C D
32	A B C D	42	A B C D
33	A B C D	43	A B C D
34	A B C D	44	A B C D
35	A B C D	45	A B C D
36	A B C D	46	A B C D
37	A B C D	47	A B C D
38	A B C D	48	A B C D
39	A B C D	49	A B C D
40	A B C D	50	A B C D

No.	ANSWER	No.	ANSWER
51	A B C D	61	A B C D
52	A B C D	62	A B C D
53	A B C D	63	A B C D
54	A B C D	64	A B C D
55	A B C D	65	A B C D
56	A B C D	66	A B C D
57	A B C D	67	A B C D
58	A B C D	68	A B C D
59	A B C D	69	A B C D
60	A B C D	70	A B C D

Part 4

No.	ANSWER	No.	ANSWER
71	A B C D	81	A B C D
72	A B C D	82	A B C D
73	A B C D	83	A B C D
74	A B C D	84	A B C D
75	A B C D	85	A B C D
76	A B C D	86	A B C D
77	A B C D	87	A B C D
78	A B C D	88	A B C D
79	A B C D	89	A B C D
80	A B C D	90	A B C D

No.	ANSWER
91	A B C D
92	A B C D
93	A B C D
94	A B C D
95	A B C D
96	A B C D
97	A B C D
98	A B C D
99	A B C D
100	A B C D

READING SECTION

Part 5

No.	ANSWER	No.	ANSWER
101	A B C D	111	A B C D
102	A B C D	112	A B C D
103	A B C D	113	A B C D
104	A B C D	114	A B C D
105	A B C D	115	A B C D
106	A B C D	116	A B C D
107	A B C D	117	A B C D
108	A B C D	118	A B C D
109	A B C D	119	A B C D
110	A B C D	120	A B C D

No.	ANSWER
121	A B C D
122	A B C D
123	A B C D
124	A B C D
125	A B C D
126	A B C D
127	A B C D
128	A B C D
129	A B C D
130	A B C D

Part 6

No.	ANSWER
131	A B C D
132	A B C D
133	A B C D
134	A B C D
135	A B C D
136	A B C D
137	A B C D
138	A B C D
139	A B C D
140	A B C D

No.	ANSWER
141	A B C D
142	A B C D
143	A B C D
144	A B C D
145	A B C D
146	A B C D
147	A B C D
148	A B C D
149	A B C D
150	A B C D

Part 7

No.	ANSWER	No.	ANSWER
151	A B C D	161	A B C D
152	A B C D	162	A B C D
153	A B C D	163	A B C D
154	A B C D	164	A B C D
155	A B C D	165	A B C D
156	A B C D	166	A B C D
157	A B C D	167	A B C D
158	A B C D	168	A B C D
159	A B C D	169	A B C D
160	A B C D	170	A B C D

No.	ANSWER	No.	ANSWER
171	A B C D	181	A B C D
172	A B C D	182	A B C D
173	A B C D	183	A B C D
174	A B C D	184	A B C D
175	A B C D	185	A B C D
176	A B C D	186	A B C D
177	A B C D	187	A B C D
178	A B C D	188	A B C D
179	A B C D	189	A B C D
180	A B C D	190	A B C D

No.	ANSWER
191	A B C D
192	A B C D
193	A B C D
194	A B C D
195	A B C D
196	A B C D
197	A B C D
198	A B C D
199	A B C D
200	A B C D